THE LAST
TEMPTATION
OF DR DALTON

BY
ROBIN GIANNA

Published in Great Britain 2014
by Mills & Boon, an imprint of Harlequin (UK) Limited,
Large Print edition 2014
Eton House, 18-24 Paradise Road,
Richmond, Surrey, TW9 1SR

© 2014 Robin Gianakopoulos

ISBN: 978-0-263-23906-5

Harlequin (UK) Limited's policy is to use papers that are natural, renewable and recyclable products and made from wood grown in sustainable forests. The logging and manufacturing processes conform to the legal environmental regulations of the country of origin.

Printed and bound in Great Britain
by CPI Antony Rowe, Chippenham, Wiltshire

After completing a degree in journalism, working in the advertising industry, then becoming a stay-at-home mum, **Robin Gianna** had what she calls her mid-life awakening. She decided she wanted to write the romance novels she'd loved since her teens, and embarked on that quest by joining RWA, Central Ohio Fiction Writers, and working hard at learning the craft.

She loves sharing the journey with her characters, helping them through obstacles and problems to find their own happily-ever-afters. When not writing, Robin likes to create in her kitchen, dig in the dirt, and enjoy life with her tolerant husband, three great kids, drooling bulldog and grouchy Siamese cat.

To learn more about her work visit her website: www.RobinGianna.com

A recent title by Robin Gianna:

CHANGED BY HIS SON'S SMILE

DEDICATION

Mom, you always told me
how important writers are to the world.

This one's for you.

ACKNOWLEDGEMENTS

Many thanks to:

Critique partner, writer friend
and pediatric emergency physician Meta
Carroll, MD, for spending so much time
walking me through medical scenes and
double-checking them for accuracy.
I appreciate it so, so much!

My sister-in-law, Trish Connor, MD,
for helping me figure out why my heroine
had needed plastic surgery as a child.

Cynthia Adams, piano teacher extraordinaire,
for the perfect music choices in the story.

CHAPTER ONE

IT WAS ALL she could do not to throw her stupid phone out of the car window.

Why wasn't he answering? Charlotte Edwards huffed out a breath and focused on driving as fast as she possibly could—not an easy task on the potholed dirt road that was just muddy enough to send her sliding into a tree if she wasn't careful.

Thank goodness it was only May in Liberia, West Africa, and just the beginning of the rainy season. Her battered four-by-four handled the terrible roads pretty well, but once they were inches deep with mud and water all bets were off.

Adrenaline surging, Charlie cautiously pressed harder on the gas pedal. No matter how uncomfortable it would make her feel, she absolutely had to catch Trent Dalton at the airport before he left—then tell him off for not answering his phone. If he had, she'd have paid for a taxi to bring him back stat to her little hospital, instead of wasting time making this trek both ways.

The sudden ringing of her phone made her jump and she snatched it up, hoping it was Trent, seeing she'd called a dozen times. "So you finally decided to look at your phone?"

"It's Thomas."

The hospital technician sounded surprised and no wonder. Her stomach twisted with dread, hoping he wasn't delivering bad news. "Sorry. You calling with an update?"

"The boy is still holding his own. I pray he'll be okay until Dr. Dalton gets back here. But I wanted to tell you that Dr. Smith has offered to do the appendectomy."

"What? Tell him no way. I'm not having a liar and a hack working on any of our patients—unless Trent's already gone, in which case we'll have no choice but to reconsider. I'll let you know as soon as I get to the airport."

"Yes, Ma."

She hung up and shook her head, managing a little smile. The word "Ma" was used as a sign of respect in Liberia, and no matter how many times she'd asked Thomas just to call her Charlie, or Charlotte, he never did.

Dr. Smith had been sent by the Global Physicians Coalition to work at the Henry and Louisa

Edwards Mission Hospital for a one-year commission. But when his arrival had been delayed they'd asked Trent to fill in for the five days until Smith could get there. Though he'd just finished a stint in India, Trent had thankfully not minded his vacation being delayed until Smith showed up.

Not long after Trent had left to start his vacation, though, the GPC called to tell her they had discovered that Smith had falsified his credentials. No way would she have him work here now.

And, because problems came in multiples, they had a very sick little boy whose life just might depend on getting surgery pronto. If only John Adams, her right-hand man for everything to do with the hospital and school, hadn't been off getting supplies today. Charlie would've sent him to drag Trent back to take care of the little boy, saving her from enduring an hour's drive in close quarters with the man. That was, if he hadn't flown off to wherever he was going next.

Anxiety ratcheting up another notch, Charlie almost called Trent again, knowing there was little point. Then she spotted the airport in the distance. Shoving down the gas pedal, hands sweating, she slithered and bumped her way down the road, parked nearly sideways and ran inside.

Relief at seeing him still sitting there nearly made her knees weak. And, of course, that weakness had nothing to do with again seeing the gorgeous man she'd enjoyed a one-night stand with just hours ago. Memories of what they'd spent the night doing filled her cheeks with hot embarrassment, and she wished with all her being she'd known their last kiss this morning wouldn't really be goodbye. She wished she had known before she'd fallen into bed with him. If she had, she most definitely would have resisted the delicious taste of his mouth and the all too seductive smile.

He was slouched in a hard chair, his long legs stretched out in front of him, a Panama hat pulled over his face with just his sensuous lips visible. Lips that had touched every inch of her body, mortified heat rushed back to her face. Even sitting, his height made him stand out among the passengers sprawled everywhere in the airport. A battered leather bag sat next to his feet. His arms were folded across his chest and he looked sound asleep.

Dang it, this was all too awkward. She squirmed

with discomfort at the very same time her nerve-endings tingled at the pleasure of seeing him again. Disgusted with herself, she took a deep breath, stepped closer and kicked his shoe. "Wake up. We need to talk."

She saw him stiffen, but other than that he didn't move, obviously pretending he hadn't heard her. What—he thought she'd come all this way just to kiss him goodbye again? Been there, done that and now it was over between them. This was about business, not pleasure. But with that thought instantly came other thoughts. Thoughts of all the pleasure she'd enjoyed with him last night, which made her even more annoyed with herself.

"I know you're not asleep, Trent Dalton. Look at me." She kicked him in the ankle this time, figuring that was sure to get his attention.

"Ow, damn it." He yanked back his leg and his finger inched up the brim of his hat until she could see the nearly black hair waving across his forehead. His light blue eyes looked at her, cautious and wary. "What are you doing here, Charlotte?"

"I'm here because you wouldn't answer your stupid cell phone."

"I turned it off. I'm on vacation."

"If you'd left it on, I wouldn't have had to spend an hour driving here, worried I wouldn't catch you before you left. We have to talk."

"Listen." His expression became pained. "It was great being with you, and moving on can be hard, you know? But going through a long-drawn-out goodbye will just make it all tougher."

"We can't say goodbye just yet."

"I'm sorry, Charlotte. I have to leave. I promise you'll be fine."

Of all the arrogant… Did he really think women had a hard time getting over him after one night of fun? Fabulous fun, admittedly, but still. She felt like conking him on the head. "Sorry, but you have to come back."

"I can't," he said in a soft and gentle voice, his blue eyes now full of pity and remorse. "We both knew we only had one night together. Tomorrow will be better. It will. In a few weeks, you'll forget all about me."

"You are so incredibly full of yourself." She couldn't control a laugh that ended in a little snort. The man was unbelievable. "Our fling was over the second you kissed me goodbye, tipped your hat and left with one of your adorable smiles and the "maybe see ya again some-time, babe" parting remark. What would make you think I had a problem with that? That's not why I'm here."

He stared at her, and she concentrated on keeping her expression nonchalant, even amused. She wasn't about to give him even a hint that she would think about him after he was gone.

"So why are you here, then?"

"I'm throwing out the new surgeon."

"Throwing him out?" Trent sat up straight. "What do you mean?"

"The GPC contacted me to tell me they found he'd falsified his credentials. That he'd had his license suspended in the U.S. for alcohol and drug use—over-prescribing of narcotics."

"Damn, so he's a loose cannon." He frowned. "But that doesn't mean he's not a good surgeon."

"Just because we're in the middle of West Africa doesn't mean our docs shouldn't be top notch. The GPC left it up to me whether I wanted him to work for us or not. And I refuse to have someone that unethical, maybe even doped up, working on our patients."

"So when is the GPC sending a new surgeon?"

"As soon as possible. They think they can get

someone temporary like you were in a few days, no more than a week. Then they'll round up a doc who can be here for the year. All you have to do is come back until the temp gets here, or a day or two before."

"I can't. I just spent a solid year in India and I need a break before I start my new job in the Philippines. I have vacation plans I can't change."

She had to wonder what woman those plans might be with. "I don't believe your vacation is more important to you than your job."

"Hey, the only reason I worked twelve straight months was to pay for my vacation."

"Yeah, right." She made a rude sound in her throat. "Like you couldn't make tons more money as a surgeon in the U.S., paying for vacations and country club memberships and fancy cars. Nobody works in a mission hospital for the money."

"Maybe I couldn't get a job in the U.S." His normally laughing eyes were oddly serious.

"Mmm-hmm." She placed her hands on the arms of his seat and leaned forward, her nose nearly touching his. The clean, manly scent of him surrounded her, making her heart go into a stupid, accelerated pit-pat. But she wasn't about to back down. "So, I never did ask—why *do* you work exclusively in tiny hospitals all over the world, pulling up stakes every year? Most docs work for the GPC part-time."

"Running from the law." His lips were so close, his breath touching her skin, and more than anything she wanted to close that small gap and kiss him one more time. "Murdered my last girlfriend after she followed me to the airport."

She had to chuckle even as she watched his eyes darken, showing he still felt the same crazy attraction she felt. That she'd felt the first second she'd met him. "I always knew you were a dangerous man, Trent Dalton. I just didn't realize quite how dangerous."

Just as she felt herself leaning in, about to kiss his sexy mouth against her will, she managed to mentally smack herself. Straightening, she stepped back.

"So. We have an immediate problem that can't wait for you to think about whether playing golf or chasing skirts, or whatever you do on vacation, is more important than my little hospital."

"What problem?"

"We've got a seven-year-old boy who's got a hot appendix. Thomas is afraid it will rupture and says he doesn't have the skill to handle it."

"Why does he think it's his appendix? Even if it is, Thomas is a well-trained tech. I was impressed as hell at the great job he does on hernias."

"Hernias aren't the same thing as an appendix, which I think you know, Dr. Dalton. Thomas says he's sure that's what it is—that you're the only one who can do it. And to tell you that the last thing the kid needs is to get septic."

His brow lowered in thought before he spoke. "What are his symptoms?"

"His mother says he hasn't eaten for two days. He's been feverish—temp of one-hundred-point-four—and vomiting."

"Belly ache and vomiting? Maybe it's just the flu."

"The abdominal pain came first, then the vomiting."

"Has the pain moved?"

"From his umbilicus to right lower quadrant." She slapped her hands back onto the chair arms. Was the man going to ask questions all day in the hope of still getting away from here? "Listen, Trent. It's been thirty-six hours. If the appendix doesn't come out, it's going to rupture. I don't need to tell you the survival rates of peritonitis in this part of the world."

A slow smile spread across Trent's face before he laughed. "Maybe *you* should do the surgery. Why the hell didn't you become a doctor?"

"I can get doctors. I can't get somebody to run that hospital. So are you coming?"

He just looked at her, silent, his amusement now gone. The worry on his face touched her heart, because she was pretty sure it was on her behalf—that he didn't want to come back because she might get hurt, which she'd bet had happened often enough in his life as a vagabond doctor.

As though it had a mind of its own, her palm lifted to touch his cheek. "I've only known you a few days, but that's enough time to realize you're a man of honor. I'm sure you'll come take care of this little boy and stick it out until we can get someone else. A one-night fling was all it was meant to be for either of us—anything more would be pointless and messy. From now on, our relationship is strictly professional. So let's go before the boy gets sicker."

His hand pressed against the back of hers, held it a moment against his cheek then lowered it to gently set her away from him. "You're good, I'll give you that." He unfolded from the chair and stood, looking down at her. "But I can only stay a few more days, so don't be trying to guilt me into more than that. I mean it."

"Agreed." She stuck out her hand to seal the deal, and he wrapped his long, warm fingers around hers. She gave his hand a quick, brisk shake then yanked her own loose but didn't manage to erase the imprint of it.

It was going to be a long couple of days.

As the car bounced in and out of ruts on the way back to the hospital, Trent glanced at the fascinating woman next to him while she concentrated on her driving. The shock of seeing Charlotte's beautiful face at the airport had nearly knocked the wind out of him. The face he'd seen all morning as he'd waited to get away from it.

He stared at her strong, silky eyebrows, lowered in concentration over eyes as green as a Brazilian rainforest. Her thick brown hair touched with streaks of bronze flowed over her shoulders, which were exposed by the sleeveless shirts she liked to wear. He nearly reached to slide his fingers over that pretty skin, and to hell with distracting her from driving.

He sucked in a breath and turned his attention back to the road. How could one night of great sex have seemed like something more than the simple, pleasant diversion it was supposed to have been?

"The road is worst these last couple miles, so hang on to your hat," she said, a smile on the pink lips whose imprint he'd still been feeling against his own as he'd sat in that damned airport for hours.

"You want me to drive?"

"Uh, no. We'd probably end up around a tree. You stick with doctoring and let me handle everything else."

He chuckled. The woman sure took her role as hospital director seriously, and to his surprise he enjoyed it. How had he never known he liked bossy women?

"So, where were you headed?" Charlotte asked.

"Florence." But for once he hadn't known what the hell he was going to do with himself for the three weeks the GPC gave doctors off between jobs. Getting in touch with one of his old girlfriends and spending time with her, whoever it might be, in London, Thailand or Rio until his next job began was how he always spent his vacation.

"Alone? Never mind. Pretend I didn't ask."

"Yeah, alone." She probably wouldn't believe it, but it was true. He hadn't called anyone. He couldn't conjure the interest, which was damned annoying. So he'd be spending three weeks in Italy all by his lonesome, with too much time to think about the fiery woman sitting next to him. The woman with the sweet, feminine name who preferred going by the name of a man.

Charlotte. Charlie. If only he could have three weeks of warms days and nights filled with her in Florence, Rome and the Italian Riviera—with her sharp mind, sense of humor and gorgeous, touchable body. Last night had been… He huffed out a breath and stared out of the window. Not a good idea to let his thoughts go any further about *that* right now.

At least there hadn't been a big, dramatic goodbye. Seeing tears in those amazing green eyes of hers and a tremble on her kissable lips would have made him feel like crap. He had to make sure that during the next few days he kept his distance so there would be no chance of that happening. Which wouldn't be easy, since he'd like nothing more than to get her into bed again.

He looked out over the landscape of lush green hills and trees that led to the hospital compound and realized he hadn't got round to asking Charlotte how she'd ended up here. "You never did tell me how your family came to be missionaries in Liberia. To build all this."

"My great-grandparents were from North Carolina. My great-grandfather came from a family of schoolteachers and missionaries, and I'm told that when he and his new wife were barely twenty they decided to head to Africa to open a school. They came to Liberia because English is the primary language. Three generations later, we're still here."

"They built the whole compound at once?" The hard work and commitment so many missionaries had put into their projects around the world amazed him.

"The hospital came about twenty years after they built the house and school in 1932. I've always loved the design of that house." She gave him a smile. "Since Liberia was founded by freed slaves, my great-grandparents brought the Southern antebellum style with them. Did you know that antebellum isn't really an architectural style, though? That in Latin it means 'before war'? It refers to homes built before the U.S. Civil War. Sadly ironic, isn't it? That the same could be said for here in Liberia too." She was talking fast, then blushed cutely. "And you probably didn't want or need a history lesson."

"Ironic's the word," he said, shaking his head. "I've never worked here before. What the civil wars have done to this country is… Heck, you can't begin to measure it."

"I know. Unbelievable how many people died. What the rest have had to live with—the chaos and terror, the shambles left behind. The horrible, disfiguring injuries." Her voice shook with anger, her lips pressed in a tight line. "Anyway, nothing can fix the past. All we can do is try to make a difference now."

"So, your great-grandparents moved here?" he prompted.

A smile banished her obvious outrage. "Apparently my great-grandmother said she'd only move here if she could make it a little like home. They built the house, filled it with beautiful furniture and even got the piano that's still in the parlor."

"And Edwardses have been here since then? What about the wars?"

"The wars forced my parents to leave when I was little and go back to the U.S. Eventually we moved to Togo to start a new mission. The hospital and school here were badly damaged by gunfire and shrapnel, but the house was just in bad disrepair, stripped of things like the windows and sinks. John Adams and I have been fixing it up, but it's third on the list of priorities."

He couldn't imagine how much work—and money—it was taking to make that happen. "So what made you want to resurrect all this? It's not like you really remember living here."

"Just because I haven't lived here until now doesn't mean my roots aren't here, and John Adams's roots. They are. They're dug in deep through our ancestors, and I intend to keep them here. My plan is to grow them, expand them, no matter what it takes."

"No matter what it takes? That's a pretty strong statement." He'd met plenty of people committed to making things better for the underprivileged, but her attitude was damned impressive.

"These people deserve whatever it takes to get them the help they need." Her grim tone lightened as they pulled in front of the one-story, painted cement hospital. "Let's get the boy fixed up. And, Trent…" Her green eyes turned all soft and sweet and he nearly reached for her. "Thanks for coming back. I promise you won't be sorry."

CHAPTER TWO

THOMAS HOVERED IN the clinic outside the door to the OR, looking anxious. "Where is the patient?" Trent asked. "Is he prepped and ready, or do you want me to examine him first?"

"I thought he should be examined again, to confirm my diagnosis. But he's in the OR. With Dr. Smith."

"Dr. Smith?" Charlie asked. What the heck was he doing in there? Hadn't she asked him to stay out of the hospital and away from patients? "Why? Did you tell him Dr. Dalton was coming back?"

"Said since he was here and the boy needs surgery fast he'd take care of it."

Anger welled up in Charlie's chest at the same time she fought it down. She supposed she should give Smith kudos for stepping up despite the circumstances, instead of being mad at her refusal to let him work there. "Well, that's…nice of him, but I'll tell him our other surgeon is here now."

"Give me a minute to scrub," Trent said as he grabbed a gown and mask and headed to the sink.

Charlie hurried into the OR to find Don Smith standing over the patient who was being attended to by the nurse anesthetist but not yet asleep. She stopped short and stared at the anxious-looking little boy. Could there be some confusion, and this wasn't the child with the hot appendix? His eyelid and eyebrow had a red, disfiguring, golf ball-sized lump that nearly concealed his eye completely. How in the world could he even see?

Her chest tightened and her stomach balled in a familiar pain that nearly made her sick. The poor child looked freakish and she knew all too well how horribly he must be teased about it. How terrible that must make him feel.

She lifted a hand to her ear, now nearly normal-looking after so many years of disfigurement. Her hand dropped to her side, balled into a fist. How wrong that he'd lived with this, when a kid in the States never would have. More proof that the project so dear to her heart was desperately needed here.

"Is this the child with appendicitis?" At Dr. Smith's nodded response, she continued. "I appreciate you being willing to take care of this emergency, but my other surgeon is here now. Help yourself to breakfast in the kitchen, if you haven't already."

"I'm here. Might as well let me operate. You'll see that I'm a capable and trustworthy surgeon. I want you to change your mind."

"I won't change my mind. Losing your license and falsifying your credentials is a serious matter, which frankly shows me you're *not* trustworthy."

"Damn it, I need this job." Smith turned to her, his face reddening with anger. "I told everyone I'd left to do humanitarian work. If I don't stay here, they'll know."

"So the only reason you want to work here is to save your reputation?" Charlie stared at him. "Hate to break it to you, but your drug addiction and loss of license is already public record in the States."

"For those who've looked. A lot of people I know haven't."

"I'm sorry, Dr. Smith, but you'll have to leave. Now."

"I'm doing this surgery and that's all there is to it. Nurse, get the anesthesia going." He turned to the patient and, without another word, began to swab the site while the child stared at him, his lip trembling.

Anger surged through her veins. Who did this guy think he was? The jerk wouldn't have spoken to her like this if she'd been a man. "Janice, don't listen to him. Stop this instant, Dr. Smith. I insist—"

Trent stepped between Charlie and Smith, grasping the man's wrist and yanking the cotton from his hand. "Maybe you didn't hear the director of this hospital. You're not doing surgery here."

"Who the hell are you?" Smith yanked his arm from Trent's grasp. "You can't tell me what to do."

"No, but she can. And I work for her." Trent had a good three inches on the man, and his posture was aggressive, his usually warm and laughing eyes a cold, steely blue. "I know your instincts as a doctor want what's best for this boy, which is immediate attention to his problem. Your being in here impedes that. So leave."

Smith began to sputter until his gaze met Trent's. He stepped back and looked away, ripping off his gown and mask and throwing them to the floor. "I can't believe a crappy little hospital in the middle of nowhere is too stupid to know how good I am. Your loss."

He stalked out and Charlie drew in a deep, slightly shaky breath of relief. She'd thought for a minute that Trent would have to physically take the guy out, and realized she'd completely trusted him to do exactly that. Then she pulled up short at the thought. She was in charge of this place and she couldn't rely on anyone else to deal with tough situations.

"Thanks, but you didn't need to do that. I had it handled."

Trent looked down at her with raised brows. "Did you, boss lady?"

"Yeah, I did."

He reached out, his long-fingered hand swiping across her shoulder, and she jerked, quickly looking down. "What, is there a bug on me?"

"No—a real big chip. I was wondering what put it there." His lips tipped up as his eyes met hers.

What? Ridiculous. "I don't have a chip on my shoulder. I'm just doing my job."

"Accepting help is part of being head honcho, you know." Those infuriatingly amused eyes lingered on her before he turned to the nurse. "Have you administered any anesthesia yet?"

"No, doctor."

"Good." He rolled a stool to the gurney and sat, that full smile now charmingly back on his face as he drew the sheet further down the child's hips. "So, buddy, where's it hurt?"

He pointed, and Trent gently pressed the top of the boy's stomach, slowly moving his hand downward to the right lower quadrant.

"Ow." The boy grimaced and Trent quit pressing his flesh to give the child's skinny chest a gentle pat.

"Okay. We're going to fix you up so it doesn't hurt any more. What's your name?"

"Lionel." The child, looking more relaxed than when Charlie had first come into the room, studied Trent. With his small index finger, Lionel pushed his bulging, droopy eyelid upward so he could see. "My belly will be all better? For true?"

"For true." Trent's smile deepened, his eyes crinkled at the corners as his gaze touched Charlie's for a moment before turning back to the child. "Inside your body, your appendix is about the size of your pinky finger. It's got a little sick and swollen, and that's what's making your belly hurt. I'm going to fix it all up while you sleep, and when you wake up it won't hurt any more. Okay?"

"Okay." Lionel nodded and smiled, showing a missing front tooth.

"But, before we take care of your sore belly, I want to talk about your eye." Trent gently moved the boy's hand before his own fingers carefully touched all around the protrusion on and above the eyelid. "Can you tell me how long it's been like this?"

Lionel shrugged. "I'nt know."

"I bet it's hard to see, huh?"

"Uh-huh. I can't see the football very well when we're kicking around. Sometimes Mommy has tape, though, and when she sticks it on there to hold it up that helps some."

"I'm sure you look tough that way. Scare your opponents." Trent grinned, and Lionel grinned back. "But I bet you could show how tough a player you are even more if you could see better."

Charlie marveled at the trusting expression on the child's face, how unquestioning he seemed as he nodded and smiled. She shifted her attention to Trent and saw that his demeanor wasn't just good bedside manner. The man truly liked kids, and that realization ratcheted the man's appeal even higher. And Lord knew he didn't need that appeal ratcheted up even a millimeter.

"Is your mother around? Or someone I can talk to about fixing it at the same time we fix your belly?"

"My mommy brought me. But I don't know where she is right now."

As his expression began to get anxious again, Trent leaned in close with a smile that would have reassured even the most nervous child. "Hey, we'll find her. Don't worry."

He stood and took a few steps away with a nod to Charlie. When they were out of hearing distance, he spoke in an undertone. "I want to take care of his hemangioma and we might as well do it while he's under for the appendix. There'll be a lot of bleeding to control, and I'll get him started on antibiotics first. After I remove the tumor, I'll decide if it's necessary to graft skin from his thigh to make it look good. In the States, you wouldn't do a clean surgery and an appendix at the same time, but I can do it with no problems."

"If it wouldn't be done in the States, we're not doing it here." Didn't he get that this was why she'd thrown Smith out?

"If you think mission doctors don't do things

we wouldn't do in the U.S., you have a lot to learn." No longer amused, a hint of steel lurked within the blue of his eyes. "Here, I can follow my gut and do what's best for the patient, and only what's best for the patient. I don't have to worry about what an insurance company wants, or cover my ass with stupid protocol. You can either trust me to know I'm doing what's best for Lionel, or not. Your call."

Charlie glanced at the boy and knew better than anyone that they were talking about a tremendously skilled procedure, one that would require the kind of detailed work and suturing a general surgeon wouldn't be capable of. "I'm in the process of getting a plastic surgery center together. That's what the new wing of the hospital is for. How about we suggest to his mommy that she bring him back when it's operational?"

He shook his head. "First, there's a good chance they live far away and it won't be easy to get back here. Second, he's probably had this a long time. The longer we wait, the more likely the possibility of permanent blindness. Even if it is fixed later, if his brain gets used to not receiving signals from the eye that part of his brain will die, and that'll be it for his vision. Not to mention that in West Africa a person is more susceptible to getting river blindness or some other parasitic infection in the eye. What if that happened and he ended up blind in both eyes? Not worth the risk."

"But can you do it? Without him still looking…bad? The plastic surgery center will be open soon. And a plastic surgeon would know how to do stuff like this better than you would."

"You don't know who you're dealing with here." His eyes held a mocking laugh. "He'll look great, I promise."

She stared at him, at his ultra-confident expression, the lazy smile. Would she be making a mistake to let him fix the hemangioma when in just a few weeks she was supposed to have a plastics specialist on board?

She looked back at Lionel, his finger still poked into the disfiguring vascular tumor so he could see out of that eye as he watched them talk. She looked at the trusting and hopeful expression on his small face. A face marred by a horrible problem Trent promised he could fix.

"Okay. You've convinced me. Do it."

CHAPTER THREE

HOURS PASSED WHILE Trent worked on Lionel. Worry over whether or not she'd made the right decision made it difficult for Charlie to sit in her office and do paperwork, but she had to try. With creditors demanding a big payment in three weeks, getting that funding check in her pocket for the new wing from the Gilchrist Foundation was critical.

She made herself shuffle through everything one more time. It seemed the only things that had to happen to get the money were a final inspection from a Gilchrist Foundation representative and proof she had a plastic surgeon on board. Both of which would happen any day now, thank heavens.

So how, in the midst of this important stuff, could she let her attention wander? She was thinking instead about the moment five days ago when Trent had strolled into this office. Thinking about how she'd stared, open-mouthed, like a schoolgirl.

Tall and lean, with slightly long, nearly black hair starkly contrasting with the color of his eyes, he was the kind of man who made a woman stop and take a second look. And a third. Normally, eyes like his would be called ice-blue, but they'd been anything but cold; warm and intelligent, they'd glinted with a constant touch of amusement. A charming, lopsided smile had hovered on his lips.

When she'd shaken his hand, he'd surprised her by tugging her against him in a warm embrace. Disarmed, she'd found herself wanting to stay there longer than the brief moment he'd held her close. She'd found her brain short-circuiting at the feel of his big hands pressed to her back; his lean, muscled body against hers; his distinctive masculine scent.

That same friendly embrace had been freely given to every woman working in the hospital, young and old, which had left all of them grinning, blushing and nearly swooning.

No doubt, the man was dynamite in human form, ready to blast any woman's heart to smithereens.

But not Charlie's. She'd known the second he'd greeted her with that genial hug that she would have to throw armor over that central organ. She'd cordially invited him to join her and John Adams for dinners, enjoying his intelligence, his amusing stories and, yes, his good looks and sophistication. She'd been sure she had everything under control.

But the night before he was to leave, when that embrace had grown longer and more intimate, when he'd finally touched his lips to hers, she hadn't resisted the desire to be with him, to enjoy a light and fun evening. An oh-so-brief diversion amidst the work that was her life. And, now that circumstances required they be in close contact for a little longer, there was no way she'd let him know that simply looking at him made her fantasize about just one more night. That was not going to happen—period.

Yes, their moment together was *so* last week. She smirked at the thought, even though a ridiculous part of her felt slightly ego-crushed that he, too, wanted to steer clear of any possible entanglement.

But that was a good thing. The man clearly loved women, all women. She'd known she was just one more notch in his travel bag, and he'd been just another notch in the fabric of her life too. Except that there hadn't been too many opportunities for "notching" since she'd finished grad school and come back to Africa.

She had to grin as she grabbed the info she wanted to share with the teachers at the school. Notching: now there was a funny euphemism for great sex if ever there was one.

She was so deep in thought about the great sex she'd enjoyed last night that she stepped into the hall without looking and nearly plowed her head into Trent's strong biceps.

"Whoa." His hands grasped her shoulders as she stumbled. "You late for lunch or something?"

Her heart sped up annoyingly as he held her just inches from his chest. "Is that a crack about how much I like to eat?"

"Not a crack. I've just observed that when you're hungry you don't let anything get between you and that plate."

She looked up into his twinkling blue eyes. "Hasn't anyone ever told you that women don't like people implying they're gluttons?"

"No negative implications from me. I like a woman who eats." His voice dropped lower. "I like the perfect and beautiful curves on your perfect and beautiful body."

As she stared up at him, the light in his eyes changed, amusement fading into something darker, more dangerous.

Desire. It hung between them, electric and heavy in the air, and Trent slowly tipped his head towards hers.

He was going to kiss her. The realization sent her heart into an accelerated tempo. A hot tingle slipped across her skin as his warm breath touched her mouth, and she lifted her hands to his chest, knowing she should push him away, but instead keeping her palms pressed to his hard pecs.

She couldn't let it happen, only to say goodbye again in a few more days. He'd made it clear he felt the same way. But, as she was thinking all that, she licked her lips in silent invitation.

His hands tightened on her arms as though he couldn't decide whether to pull her close or push her away, then he released her. "Sorry. I shouldn't have said that. I forgot we're just casual acquaintances now." He shoved his hands in his pockets, his expression now impassive, all business. "I wanted to let you know it went well with Lionel."

She sucked in a breath, trying to be equally

businesslike, unaffected by his potent nearness and the need to feel his lips on hers one more time. "He's okay? You fixed the hemangioma? And he looks good?"

"You probably wouldn't think he looks good."

Her stomach dropped. "Why...? What, is it messed up?"

He laughed. "No. But right now it's sutured and swollen and would only look good to a zombie. Or a surgeon who knows what he's doing. We'll take the bandage off in a few days."

"Okay. Great." She pressed her hand to her chest, hoping to goodness it really had turned out all right. Hoping the hard beat of her heart was just from the scare, and not a lingering effect of the almost-kiss of a moment ago.

"Can you unlock your car for me? I need to get my stuff out and take it to my room."

"Of course. But I didn't tell you—even though I'm not happy with our Dr. Smith, I couldn't exactly throw him out on the streets until his flight leaves tomorrow. So he's going to be staying in the room you were in for just tonight."

"What? I'm not staying at your house again."

It was hard not to be insulted at the horror on his face. 'Goodbye, Charlie' took on a whole new meaning with Trent. "Sorry, but you're sleeping on a rollaway here in my office. I don't want you staying in my house, either."

"You do too." His lips quirked, obliterating his frown.

"Uh, no, I don't. Like I said before, you're an egomaniac. Somebody needs to bring you down a peg or two, and I guess it's going to be me."

"Thanks for your help. I appreciate it more than you know." That irritating little smile gave way to seriousness. "And it's good we're on the same page. Second goodbyes can get…sticky."

"Agreed. And you're welcome. I'll get my keys now before I head to the school." She turned, so glad she hadn't fallen into an embrace with the conceited guy. His long fingers grasped her elbow and the resulting tingle that sped up her arm had her jerking it away.

"Wait a second. You're going up to the school?"

"Yes. I have some things I want to go over with the teachers. I'm having lunch with them and the kids."

He was silent, just looking at her with a slight frown over those blue eyes, as though he couldn't decide something. He finally spoke. "Mind if I come along? I'd like to see it, and I'm not needed in the clinic right now."

"Sure. If you want." She shrugged casually. Did the man have to ponder whether seeing the school was worth being with her for a few hours? Or was she being hypersensitive?

She led the way down the short hall into the soupy, humid air, making sure to stand on Trent's left so her good ear would be closest to him. "The kids love visitors. But we'll be walking, so don't be surprised if you get a little muddy."

"Glad I'm not wearing my designer shoes today. Then again, I could've taken them off. Nothing like a little mud between the toes."

The thought of cool, squishy mud on bare feet, then playing a little footsie together, sounded strangely appealing, and she rolled her eyes at herself as they trudged up the road to the schoolhouse. Maybe she needed to try and find a local boyfriend to take off this edge she kept feeling around Trent. He reached for the binder of papers she was carrying and tucked it under his arm.

"So you were the boy who earned points by carrying a girl's books to school? Why doesn't that surprise me?"

"Hey, I looked for any way to earn points. Carrying books was just one of them."

"I can just imagine. So what other ways did you earn points?" And why couldn't she just keep her mouth shut? "You know, never mind. I don't think I want to know."

"You already know some of them." He leaned closer as they walked, the scent of him teasing her nose. "But a few things got me more points than others. For example, my famous shoulder-rubs always scored big."

The memory of that shoulder rub came in a rush of clarity—them naked in her bed, sated and relaxed, the ceiling fan sending cool whispers of air across their skin. Her breathing got a little shallow and she walked faster.

"One of the ground rules is to stop with the references to last night. Got it?"

"I wasn't referring to anything but the shoulder rub I gave you at your office desk. Can I help it if your mind wants to go other places?"

She scowled at the bland innocence on his face. The man was about as far from innocent as he could be. "Mmm-hmm. So, when you mention back rubs, you don't picture me naked?"

His slow smile, his blue eyes dancing as he

leaned closer, made her feel a little weak at the knees. "Charlotte, you can bet I frequently picture you naked." His gaze held hers, then slid away to the road. "Again, I'm sorry. That was inappropriate. Let's talk about the school. Did you open it at the same time as the hospital?"

Phew; she had to stop just blurting out what she was thinking, though he seemed to have the same problem. Good thing he changed the subject, or she just might have melted down into the mud.

"John Adams concentrated on getting the school open while I focused on the hospital. His daughter, Patience—I think you met her?—will be going to school next year, so he's been pretty excited about the project. They live in a small apartment attached to the school, so she'll probably be there today. She loves to hang out in the classrooms and pretend she can read and write."

"Patience is a cutie. She and I bonded over ice-cream." His eyes always turned such a warm blue when he talked about children; it filled her chest with some kind of feeling she didn't want to analyze. "So, is John from here?"

"Just so you know, he's always gone by both his first and last name. I'm not sure why." She smiled. "John Adams's parents both worked with my parents here. They left too when the war broke out. Their family and mine met up again in Togo and, since he's just a few years older than I am, he's kind of like a brother. And I love Patience like I would a niece."

"Where's her mother?"

"She died suddenly of meningitis. It was a terrible shock." She sighed. "Moving here with me to open this place has been a fresh start for John Adams and Patience, and hugely helpful to me. I couldn't have done it alone."

"I've been wondering where your funding is coming from. The GPC's been cutting back, so I know they can't be floating cash for the whole hospital."

"We've shaken down every possible donor, believe me. The school was as big a shambles as the hospital, and usually donor groups focus on one or the other. But we managed to get the building reasonably repaired and the basics in—desks and supplies and stuff. We opened with thirty primary-school-aged kids enrolled and have almost a hundred now." She shook her head. "It's not nearly enough, though, with half a million Liberian kids not attending school at all. And sixty percent of girls and women over fifteen can't read or write."

He frowned. "Is it as hard to raise cash for a school as it is for a hospital?"

"It's all hard. But I'm working on getting a donation from a church group in the States that'll help us hire a new teacher and have enough food for the kids' lunches. I'm excited. It looks like it's going to come through." Charlie smiled at Trent, but his expression stayed uncharacteristically serious. "We hate turning families away, but can't just endlessly accept kids into the program, you know? It's not fair to the teachers or the students to have classrooms so big nobody gets the attention they need. So I'm sure hoping it works out."

"How soon will you know?"

"In the next day or two, I think."

His expression was oddly inscrutable. "Be sure to tell me if the donation comes through or not, okay?"

"Okay." She had to wonder why he wanted to know, but appreciated his interest. "As for the hospital, I'm supposed to get a giant check from the Gilchrist Foundation as soon as the new wing is ready to go, thank heavens."

He stopped dead and stared at her. "The Gilchrist Foundation?"

"Yes. You've heard of them?"

"Yeah. You could say that."

CHAPTER FOUR

"Has the Gilchrist Foundation donated to hospitals you've worked at before?" Charlotte asked. "Did they come through with their support? I'm a little worried, because we're scraping the bottom of the barrel just to get the wing finished."

Trent looked into her sweet, earnest face before turning his attention to the verdant landscape—not nearly as vivid and riveting as the color of her eyes. "They're a reputable organization."

"That's good to hear." She sounded slightly breathless, her footsteps squishing quickly in the mud, and he slowed his stride. He resisted the urge to grasp her arm to make sure she didn't slip and fall. "I heard they were, but they're making us jump through some hoops to get it."

He almost asked *what hoops?*, but decided to keep out of it. The last thing he wanted was to get involved with anything to do with the Gilchrist Foundation. Or for Charlotte to find out his connection to it. "It'll be fine, I'm sure. So, this is it." He looked up at the one-storey cement building painted a golden yellow, the windows and door trimmed in a brick color. "Looks like you've done a nice job restoring it."

"It took a lot of money and manpower. It was basically a shell, with nothing left inside. The windows were gone and there were bullet holes everywhere. John Adams and I are pretty proud of how it turned out."

As they reached the wooden door of the school he saw Charlotte glance up at the sky, now filling with dark-gray clouds. "Looks like rain's coming, and I wasn't smart enough to bring an umbrella. Sorry. We won't stay too long."

"I'm not made of sugar, you know. I won't melt," he teased. Then the thought of sugar made him think of her sweet lips and the taste of her skin. It took a serious effort to turn away, not to pull her close to take a taste.

They left their muddy shoes outside before she led the way in. Children dressed in white shirts with navy-blue pants or skirts streamed from classrooms, laughing and chattering.

"Mr. Trent!" Cute little Patience ran across the room, the only one in a sleeveless dress instead of a uniform. "Mr. Trent, you bring me candy?"

"Sorry, Miss Impatience, I don't have any left." She wrapped her arms around his leg and the crestfallen expression on her face made him wish he'd brought a whole lot more. Too bad he hadn't known he'd be here longer than a few days.

"How about gum?"

He laughed and swung her up into his arms. "Don't have any of that left either." He lowered his voice. "But, next time you're at the hospital, I'll sneak some pudding out of the pantry for you, okay?"

"I heard that." Charlotte's brows lifted. "Since when are you two best friends? Dr Trent just got here a few days ago."

"Mr. Trent and me are good friends, yes." The girl's arms tightened around his neck, which felt nice. Kids didn't want or expect anything from you but love. And maybe candy too, he thought with a smile. There weren't too many adults he could say that about.

"Patience and I share a fondness for that chocolate pudding."

"Hmm." A mock frown creased Charlotte's face as she leaned close to them. "I didn't know you were stealing supplies, Dr Dalton. I'm going to have to keep an eye on you."

"What's the punishment for stealing?" His gaze dropped from her amused eyes to her pink lips. Maybe if he stole a kiss he'd find out.

"I don't think you want to know." Her eyes were still smiling and he found himself riveted by the glow of gold and brown flecks deep within that beautiful green.

"Miss Edwards!" Several kids ran their way. "You coming to see our play this Wednesday? Please come, Miss Edwards!"

Charlotte wrapped her arms around their shoulders in hugs, one after another, talking and smiling, making it obvious she wasn't a distant director around here; that she put in a lot of face time, truly cared about these kids. That impressed the hell out of him. He'd seen a lot of hospital directors in his day, even some in mission hospitals, who were more focused on the bottom line and making donors happy than they were about helping the patients they existed for.

Trent set Patience back on her feet. "Have you been doing any more drawing? You know I like to see your art." Nodding enthusiastically, her short legs took off running back down a hall.

He watched Charlotte with the kids. He'd never worked at a mission hospital that included a school in its compound. He hadn't been able to resist a chance to peek at it and see what they were accomplishing, even when he knew it wasn't the best idea to spend much time with Charlotte.

The whole reason he'd come was to see the school children, but he found it impossible to pull his attention from the smiling woman talking to them. He'd teased her about picturing her naked, but the truth was he couldn't get the vision of her out of his mind at all: clothed or unclothed, smiling and happy or ready to kick someone's ass.

Damn it.

Time to get his mind on the whole reason he was here—to find out what the kids were learning and how the school helped them. Charlotte patted a few of the children and turned her attention to him.

"Is this where we're going to eat?" he asked. The room was filled with folding tables that had seats attached, and some of the children were already sitting down.

"What, are you hungry? And you were making fun of me wanting lunch."

He grinned at her teasing expression. Man, she was something. A fascinating mix of energy, passion and determination all mixed in with a sweet, soft femininity. "I haven't eaten since five a.m. But I still wouldn't knock someone over in a hall-way in search of a meal."

"As if I could knock you over, anyway." She took the binder from him and gestured to the tables. "Find a seat. I'll be right back."

Standing here, looking at all the bright-eyed and happy kids, he was annoyed with himself. Why hadn't it hadn't ever occurred to him to do-nate some of his fortune to this kind of school? He'd focused on giving most of his anonymous donations to the kind of hospitals he worked in. To those that medically served the neediest of humans in the world.

But that was going to change to include helping with education—a whole other kind of poverty. Not having access to learning was every bit as bad as having no access to health care.

"Here's my picture, Mr. Trent!" Patience ran up with a piece of construction paper crayoned with smiling children sitting at desks, one of them a lot bigger than the others.

"Who's this student?" he asked, pointing at the large figure he suspected just might be a self-portrait of the artist.

"That's me." Patience gave him a huge smile.

"I sit in class sometimes now. Miss Jones said I could."

"I bet you're really smart. You'll be reading and writing in no time." And to make that happen for a lot more kids, he'd be calling his financial manager pronto.

"Yes." She nodded vigorously. "I go to read right now."

She took off again and he chuckled at how cute she was, with her little dress and pigtails flying as she ran. He sat at one of the tables and saw the kids eyeing him, some shyly, others curious, a few bold enough to come close. Time for the tried and tested icebreaker. He pulled a pack of cards from his pocket and began to shuffle. "Anybody want to see a card trick?"

Faces lit, giggles began and a few children headed over, then more shoved their way in, until the table was full and the rest stood three-deep behind them.

"Okay." He fanned the cards face down and held them out to a grinning little girl with braids all over her head. "Pick a card. Any card." When she began to pull one out, he yanked the deck away. "Not that one!"

Startled, her grin faded and she stared at him.

"Just kidding." He gave her a teasing smile to let her know it was all in fun, and she giggled in relief as the other children hooted and laughed. He held out the fanned deck again. "Pick a card. I won't pull it away again, honest. Look at it, show it to a friend, but don't let me see it. Then stick it back in the deck."

The girl dutifully followed his directions. He did his sleight-of-hand shuffling before holding up a card. "Is this it?" He had to grin at how crestfallen they looked as they shook their heads. "Hmm. This it?"

"No, that's not it." She looked worried, like it would somehow be her fault if the trick didn't work.

"Well, you know third time's a charm, right? *This* is the one you picked." He held up what he knew would be the card she'd chosen, and everyone shrieked and whooped like he'd pulled a rabbit from a hat or held up a pot of gold.

"How you do that, mister?" a boy asked, craning his neck at the card deck as though the answer was written there.

"Magic." One of the best parts about doing the trick was showing the kids how to do it themselves. "How about we do it a few more times? Then I'll teach you exactly how it's done."

Before Charlie and the teachers even got back to the common room, the sound of loud talking and laughter swept through the school's hall. Mariam, the headmistress, pursed her lips and frowned. "I'm sorry, Miss Charlotte. I don't know why they're being so rowdy. I'll take care of it."

"It's fine. They're at lunch, after all." Though she was pretty sure it hadn't been served yet. Curious as to what was causing all the excitement, she walked into the room, only to stop in utter surprise at the scene.

Looking ridiculously large for it, Trent sat at a table completely surrounded by excited children, like some handsome Pied Piper. He was holding up cards, shuffling and flicking them, then handing them to kids who did the same, all the while talking and grinning. As she came farther into the room, she could hear the students bombarding him with questions that he patiently answered more than once.

She hadn't seen this side of Trent before. Yes, she'd seen his gentle bedside manner with Lionel, his obvious caring for the boy. Still, she couldn't help but be amazed at the connection she was witnessing. So many of the children in this school had been traumatized in one way or another and a number of them were orphaned. Yet, to watch this moment, you'd think none of them had a care in the world other than having a fun time with whatever Trent was sharing with them.

She moved closer to the table. "What's going on here?"

One of the older boys waved some cards. "Mr. Trent is showing us card tricks, Miss Edwards! See me do one!"

"I'd love to." Her eyes met Trent's and her heart fluttered a little at the grin and wink he gave her. "But you should call him Dr Trent. He's a physician working at the hospital for a few days."

"Dr Trent?" Anna, a girl in the highest grade they could currently offer, looked from Charlie to Trent, her expression instantly serious. "You a doctor? My baby brother is very sick with the malaria. Mama Grand has been treating him, but we're worried. Would you care if I go get him and bring him here for you to see?

"Can your mommy or grandmother bring him to the hospital?" Charlie asked.

Anna shook her head. "Mommy is away working in the rice fields. But I can get him and carry him there if that is better."

"How old is he?" Charlie asked.

"Six years old, Ma."

Charlie knew many of these kids walked miles to get to school, and didn't want Anna hauling an ill six-year-old that kind of distance. Not to mention that she could hear rain now drumming hard on the roof of the school. "How about if I drive and get him? You can show me where you live."

Trent stood. "It's pouring outside. I'll go back and get the car and pick you two up, then we'll just see him at your home."

Charlie pulled her keys from her pocket and headed for the door. "It's okay, I'll just…"

In two strides, Trent intercepted her and snagged the keys from her hand. "Will you just let someone else help once in a while? Please? I'll be right back."

Charlie watched as he ducked out of the doorway into the heavy rain, all too aware of the silly surge of pleasure she felt at the way he insisted on taking on this problem, never mind that she could handle it herself. Well, not the medical part; she was thankful he'd be able to contribute his expertise as well as the nurses and techs at the hospital.

Her car pulled up in no time and, before she and Anna could come out, Trent had jogged to the door with an open umbrella and ushered Anna into the backseat. Water slid down his temples and dripped from his black hair as he opened the passenger door for Charlie. "You're riding shotgun this time, boss lady."

"It's my car. I know how to drive in this kind of weather."

He made an impatient sound. "Please just get in and stop arguing."

She opened her mouth to insist, but saw his set jaw and his intent blue eyes and found herself sliding into the seat, though why she let him tell her what to do she wasn't sure. It must have something to do with the man's overwhelming mojo.

She wasn't surprised that he proved more than competent at the wheel, despite the deepening mud and low visibility through the torrential rain. Even in good weather, this thinning road was barely more than a track through the bush. It couldn't really be called a road at all at the moment.

A group of crooked, heartbreakingly dilapidated zinc shacks appeared through the misty sheets of rain, and the distinctive smell of coal fires used for cooking touched Charlie's nose.

"It's up here. That one," Anna said, pointing.

The car slid to a stop. "Sit tight for a sec," Trent said. He again grabbed the umbrella and brought it to their side of the car before opening Charlie's door.

"I'm not made of sugar, you know. I won't melt," Charlie said, repeating what he'd said to her earlier as she climbed out to stand next to him.

"You sure about that? I remember you tasting pretty sweet." Beneath the umbrella, he was so close she could feel his warmth radiating against her skin. The smell of the rain, mud, coal fires and Trent's own distinctive and appealing scent swirled around her in a sensory overload. His head dipped and those blue eyes of his met hers and held. She realized she was holding her breath, struck by a feeling of the two of them being completely alone in the world as the rain pounded a timpani concerto on the fabric above their heads.

Her heart did a little dance as his warm breath touched her face. Blue eyes darker now, his head dipped closer still until his lips slipped across hers, whisper-soft, clinging for a moment. "Yeah. Like sugar and honey."

His lids lowered in a slow blink before he straightened, turning to open Anna's door.

The child led the way as they trudged up to a group of metal shacks, giving Charlie's heart rate a chance to slow. Why had he kissed her when they'd agreed not to go there? Probably for the same reason she'd wanted him to—that overwhelming chemistry between them that had caught fire the first day they'd met.

They approached a shack that looked as though it must be Anna's home. A cooking pot sat over a coal fire with what smelled like cassava simmering inside. The shack's crooked door was partially open, and Anna shoved it hard, scraping it along the muddy ground until they could step inside the dark interior.

A young child lay sleeping on a mat on the dirt floor and another was covered with a blanket, exposing only his or her outline. An older woman with a brightly patterned scarf on her head sat on a plastic chair, stitching some fabric.

"Mama Grand, I bring a doctor to see Prince."

The woman looked at them suspiciously. "No need, Anna. I use more healing herbs today and Prince will be fine soon."

Anna twisted her fingers and looked imploringly at her. "Please. The doctor is here, so let him see if Prince is getting better."

Trent stepped forward and gave one of his irresistibly charming smiles to the woman. "I'm sure you're doing a fine job taking care of Prince. But the boss lady, Miss Edwards here, will be mad at me if I don't have work to do today. She might not even pay me. Can I please just take a look at your fine little one while I'm here?"

The woman's stern expression softened slightly, and after a moment she inclined her head. Charlie had a hard time suppressing a smile. Trust Trent to turn it around to make Charlie look like the bad guy, and to know exactly how to twist it so his being there was no reflection on the older woman's treatments.

Trent crouched down and looked back at the woman. "Is this Prince hiding under the blanket? May I look at him?"

She nodded again, and Trent reached to pull the blanket from the small, huddled shape. He quickly jerked back when he saw the exposed child.

"What the...?" Trent's face swung towards Charlie, his eyebrows practically reaching his hair.

CHAPTER FIVE

THE LITTLE BOY looked like a ghost. Literally. He'd been covered head to toe in white paint. In all Trent's years of seeing crazy and unusual things around the world, he'd never seen this.

Charlotte covered a small smile with her fingertips, and he could tell she wanted to laugh at whatever the hell his expression was. Could he help it if it startled him to see the little guy looking like that?

"It's a common home remedy here for malaria. The sick person is painted white as part of the cure."

"Ah." Trent schooled his features into normal professionalism and turned back to the boy. He touched his knuckles to the sleeping child's cheeks, then pressed the child's throat, both of which were hot and sweaty. The boy barely opened his eyes to stare at him before becoming wracked by a prolonged, dry cough. When the cough finally died down, Trent leaned close to him with a smile he hoped would reassure him. "Hi, Prince. I'm Dr Dalton. How do you feel? Anything hurting?"

Prince didn't answer, just slid his gaze towards his sister. She knelt down next to him and touched her hand to the boy's thin shoulder. "It's okay, Prince. Dr Dalton is here to help you get better."

"Have you had belly pain or diarrhea?" The boy still just stared at him, looking scared, as though Trent was the one who looked like a ghost. Maybe the child was delirious. "Anna, do you know about any belly pain? Has he been confused or acting strange?"

She nodded. "He did complain about his tummy hurting. And he has been saying silly things. I think he seems the same as when I had the malaria—shaking and feeling very hot and cold."

"Trent, how about I drive back to the compound and get the malaria medicine?" Even through the low light, he could see the green of Charlotte's eyes focused intently on his. "I'll bring it back here; maybe we won't have to scare him by taking him to the hospital."

He shook his head, not at all sure this was malaria. "If he has belly pain, it might be typhoid, which requires a different kind of antibiotic. Hard to tell with a child who's sick and obtunded like he is. The only way to know for sure is if we take him back to the hospital and get a blood test—see if it shows the parasites or not."

"No hospital." The older woman's lips thinned. "If de boy go, he will never come back."

Obviously, the poor woman had lost someone she loved. "I'll watch over him myself," Trent said. "I promise to keep him safe."

"Mama Grand, no boys are kidnapped any more. For true. The war is over a long time now."

Damn, so that was what she was worried about. He could barely fathom that boys this young had been kidnapped to be soldiers, but knew it had happened so often that some parents sent their children out of the country to be safe, never to see them again.

He stood and reached for the woman's rough and gnarled hand. "I understand your worries. But it's important that Prince have a test done that we can only do at the hospital. I promise you that I will care for Prince and look after him like I would if he were my own child, and return him to you when he's well. Will you trust me to do that?"

The suspicious look didn't completely leave the woman's face, but she finally nodded. Trent didn't want to give her a chance to change her mind and quickly gathered Prince in his arms, wrapping the blanket around him as best he could.

"You want to come with us, Anna? You don't have to, but it might make Prince feel more comfortable," Charlotte said.

"Yes. I will come."

"Are you going to hold Prince so I can drive, or do you want to take the wheel?" he asked Charlotte as they approached the car.

"You know the answer to that." Her gorgeous eyes glinted at him. "You're in the passenger seat, Dr. Dalton."

He had to grin. "You really should address this little controlling streak of yours, Ms. Edwards. Find out why relinquishing power scares you so much."

"It doesn't scare me. I just trust my own driving over anyone else's."

"Mm-hm. One of these days, trying to control the direction the world spins is going to weigh heavy on those pretty shoulders of yours. Drive on, boss lady."

Tests proved that Prince did indeed have typhoid, and after a couple days he'd recovered enough to return home. Charlie was glad that Trent's expertise had led him to insist the child be tested, instead of just assuming it was malaria, as she had.

She was also glad that, in the days that had passed since Trent had come back, she'd managed to stop thinking about him for hours at a time. Well, maybe not *hours*. Occasionally, the man sneaked into her thoughts. Not her fault, since she wasn't deaf and blind—okay, a little hard of hearing in that one ear of hers she was grateful to have it at all.

His voice, teasing and joking with the nurses and techs, sometimes drifted down the hall to her office. His distinctively tall form would occasionally stride in front of her office on his way from the clinic to the hospital ward until she decided just to shut the darn door.

She'd made a conscious effort to stay away from the hospital ward where she might run into him. She got dinner alone at home, or ate lunch at her desk so she wouldn't end up sitting with him in the kitchen. She spent time at the school instead of here, where thoughts of him kept invading her brain, knowing he was somewhere nearby.

It helped that Trent had kept their few interactions since the brief kiss in the rain short and professional. When the man said goodbye, he sure meant it, never mind that she felt the same way. Thank heavens he'd be leaving again in the next few days so she wouldn't have to suffer the embarrassment of thinking about all they'd done in their single night together.

Her door opened and her heart gave an irritating little kick of anticipation that it just might be his blue eyes she'd see when she looked up.

But it was John Adams standing there. "Any word yet on the funding for another teacher?"

She smiled and waved a paper. "Got the green light. I'm sending the final forms today, and they said we should get a check in about a month. Is the woman you've been training going to work out?"

"Yes, most definitely." He dramatically slapped a hand to his barrel chest. "She is smart and beautiful and I am in love with her. Thanks to God I can officially offer her a job."

"You're starting to remind me of ladies' man Dr Dalton. No mixing business with pleasure." A flush filled her cheeks as soon as the words were out of her mouth, since she'd done exactly that, and the pleasure had been all too spectacular.

"Yes, ma'am." He grinned. "Anyway, I also stopped to tell you to come look at our little patient this morning."

"What little patient?"

"Lionel. The one with appendicitis and the hemangioma—or who used to have a hemangioma. You won't believe what Trent's done with it."

Alarm made Charlie's heart jerk in her chest. She'd worried from the moment she'd agreed to let Trent take care of such a delicate procedure. Had he messed it up? She'd checked on the child a couple of times, but a patch had still covered his eye. "What do you mean? Is it going to have to be redone when we get a plastic surgeon in here?"

"Just come and see."

She rose and followed him to the hospital ward, her fears eased a bit by John Adams's relaxed and smiling expression. Still, she couldn't shake the feeling that she might have made a big mistake.

Lionel's head was turned towards his mother, who sat by his bedside, and Charlie found herself holding her breath as they came to stand beside him.

"Show Miss Charlotte how well you're seeing today, Lionel," John Adams said.

The boy turned his head and she stared in disbelief.

The patch had been removed and, considering he'd had surgery only days before, he looked shockingly, amazingly normal.

The angry red bulge that had been the vascular tumor was gone. His eyebrow and eyelid, other than still being bruised and slightly swollen from surgery, looked like any other child's. His big, brown eye, wide and lit with joy, was now completely visible, just like his other one.

"Oh, my. Lionel, you look wonderful!" She pressed her hands to her chest. "Can you see out of that eye?"

"I can see! Yes, I can! And Mommy show me in the mirror how handsome I look!"

"You even more handsome than your brothers now, boyo, and I told them so," his mother said with a wide smile.

Tears stung Charlie's eyes as she lifted her gaze to the child's mother and saw so many emotions on the woman's face: happiness; profound relief; deep gratitude.

All because of Trent.

Where was the man? Had he seen the amazing result of his work? She turned to a smiling

John Adams. "Has Dr Dalton seen him since the patch was removed?"

"Oh, yes. He took it off himself this morning."

"Dr. Dalton told me he gave me special powers, too, like Superman." The child's face radiated excitement. "Said I have x-ray vision now."

His mother laughed. "Yes, but Dr. Dalton was just joking and you know it. Don't be going and telling everyone that, or they'll expect you to see through walls."

"I can see so good, I bet I can see through walls. I bet I can."

"Maybe you'll become a doctor, Superman, who can see people's bones before you operate." Trent's voice vibrated into the room from behind Charlie's back. "That would be pretty cool."

"I want to be a doctor like you. I want to fix people like you do, Dr. Trent."

Trent's smile deepened as he came to stand next to Charlie. "That's a good goal, Lionel. If you study hard in school, I bet you can do anything you set your mind to."

Charlie stared at Trent, looking so relaxed, like all this was no big deal. Maybe it wasn't to him, but it was to her, and to Lionel and to his mother. A very, very big deal.

"I can't believe the wonderful job you did," she said, resting her hand on his forearm. "You told me I didn't know who I was dealing with and you were sure right."

"Now she learns this, just before I'm ready to leave."

The twinkle in his eyes, and his beautifully shaped lips curved into that smile, were practically irresistible. She again was thankful that he would be heading out of her life very soon before she made a complete fool of herself. "Good thing you don't have x-ray vision too. Hate to think what you'd use it for."

"Checking for broken bones, of course." His smile widened. "What else?"

She wasn't going where her mind immediately went. "Probably to decipher a bank-vault combination, so you could go on vacation without working a solid year. Speaking of which, the GPC says a general surgeon should be here in a matter of days, so you can have them schedule your flight out of here soon."

"Great."

The relief on his face was obvious and she hated that it hurt a tiny bit to see it. "I can't help but wonder, though, why are you working as a general surgeon when you can do things like this?"

His smile faded. "You think plastic surgery has more value? More than saving someone's life? I don't."

"It's a different kind of value: changing lives; changing the way someone is viewed, the way they view themselves. You have an obvious gift for this, a skill many would envy." Did he not see how important all that was? "Your focus should be on plastic surgery. On helping people that way."

"The way other people view a person, what they expect them to be and who they expect them to be, shouldn't have anything to do with how they view themselves." He took a step back and pulled his arm away from her touch. She hadn't known those eyes of his were capable of becoming the chilly blue that stared back at her. "Excuse me, I have a few other patients to check on."

She frowned as she watched him walk through the hospital ward. What had she said to make him mad?

"I have things to do too," John Adams said. But, like her, his gaze followed Trent, his expression thoughtful. "Bye, Lionel. See you later, Charlie."

"Okay. Listen, can you come have dinner tonight at my house? I'd like to talk to you about some things."

He nodded and headed off. Charlie watched Trent examining another patient and could only hope John Adams came up with a good idea for how she could accomplish her newest goal—which was to encourage Trent to perform surgery on a few patients in the day or two he'd still be here, patients who'd needed reconstructive surgery long before the plastic surgery wing had even been conceived.

She knew how desperately some of these people needed to have their lives changed in that way. Not to mention that it wouldn't hurt for her to have a few "before and after" photos that would impress the Gilchrist Foundation with what they were already accomplishing. And, really, how could Trent object?

As she headed back to her office, her cell phone rang and she pulled it from her pocket. "Charlotte Edwards."

"Hey, Charlie! It's Colleen. How're things going with Trent Dalton?"

"With Trent?" What the heck? Did the gossip vine go all the way to GPC headquarters? Besides, nobody here knew she and Trent had briefly hooked up...did they? "What do you mean?"

"Is it working out that he came back until the new temp gets there?"

Phew. Thank heavens she really didn't have to answer the first question, though their moment together was history anyway. "He's doing a good job, but I know he wants to move on. Do you have a final arrival date for the new doc?"

"Perry Cantwell has agreed to come and we're finalizing his travel plans. Should be any day now." Her voice got lower, conspiratorial. "Just tell me. I've seen photos of Trent that make me salivate, but is he really as hunky as everyone says? Whenever I talk to him on the phone his voice makes me feel all tingly."

If just his voice made Colleen feel tingly, Charlie hated to think what would happen if she saw him in person. She wasn't about to confess to Colleen that, despite his reputation, she'd fallen into bed with him for one more than memorable night. While she felt embarrassed about that now, she still couldn't regret it, despite unexpectedly having to work with him again. "He's all right. If you like tall, good-looking surgeons who flirt with every woman in sight and think everything's amusing."

"Mmm. Sounds good to me if the surgeon in question has beautiful black hair and gorgeous eyes." The sound of a long sigh came through the phone and Charlie shook her head. She supposed she should feel smug that über-attractive Trent had wanted to spend a night with her. But, since he likely had a woman in every port, that didn't necessarily say much about her personal sex appeal. "I actually have his new release papers on my desk to send out today. Are you going to hit on him before he leaves?" Colleen asked. "Might be a fun diversion for a couple days."

Been there, done that. And, yes, it had been—very fun. Keeping it strictly professional now, though, was the agreed goal. "I've got tons to do with the new wing opening any time now. And my dad called to say he's coming some time soon to see how things are going with that."

"Actually, I have some bad news about the new wing, I'm afraid." Colleen's voice went from light to serious in an instant.

Her heart jerked. "What bad news?"

"You know David Devor, the plastic surgeon we had lined up to work there?" Colleen asked. "He has a family emergency and can't come until it's resolved, which could be quite a while."

"Are you kidding me? You know I have to have someone here next week, Colleen! The Gilchrist Foundation made it clear we won't get the funding we need until I have at least one plastic surgeon on site."

"I know. I'm doing the best I can. But I'm having a hard time finding a plastic surgeon who wants to work in the field. I'm turning over every rock I can, but I can't promise anybody will be there until Dr. Devor is available. Sorry."

Lord, this was a disaster! Charlie swiped her hand across her forehead. The hospital was scarily deep in the red from getting the new wing built. It had to be opened pronto.

"Okay." She sucked in a calming breath. "But I have to have a plastic surgeon, like *now*."

"I know, but I just told you—"

"Listen. I need you to hold off a day or two before you send Trent's release papers. Give me time to talk to him about maybe staying on here. If he agrees, you can send Perry Cantwell somewhere else."

There was a long silence on the phone before Colleen spoke. "Why? Cantwell's expecting to come soon. And I can't just hold Trent's paperwork. He's already filled in for you twice and is way overdue for his vacation. I don't get it."

"I found out Trent's a plastic surgeon, not just a general surgeon." She gulped and forged on. "If Devor can't be here, I have to keep Trent here at least long enough to get the wing open and the funding in my hand. Otherwise I won't be able to pay the bank, and who knows what'll happen?"

"Maybe he'll agree to stay."

"Maybe. Hopefully." But she doubted he would. Hadn't he made it more than clear that he wanted to head out ASAP? The only reason he'd come back for a few days was because of how sick Lionel had been. "All I'm asking is for you to hang onto his release papers until I can talk to him."

"Charlie." Colleen's voice was strained. "You're one of my best friends. Heck, you got me this job! But you're asking me to do something unethical here."

"Of course I don't want you to do anything you feel is unethical." This was her problem, not Colleen's, and it wouldn't be right to put her friend in the middle of it. "Just send them out tomorrow instead of today, address them to me and I'll make sure he gets them. That will give me time to contact the Gilchrist Foundation and see if they'll make an exception on their requirements before the donation check is sent. If they won't, I'll try to get their representative to come right now while Trent's still here. I'm pretty sure the guy is close—somewhere in West Africa. I'll go from there."

Colleen's resigned sigh was very different from the one when she'd been swooning over Trent earlier. "All right. I'll wait until tomorrow to send the release papers and finalize Perry's travel plans to give you time to talk to Trent. But that's it."

"Thanks, Colleen. You're the best." Charlie tried to feel relieved but the enormity of the problem twisted her gut. "Hopefully they'll send the funding check even if we don't have a plastic surgeon here yet and we'll be out of the woods. I'll keep you posted."

The second she hung up, she searched for the Gilchrist Foundation's number. What would she do if they flat out said the conditions of the contract had to be met, which would probably be their response? Or if they couldn't send their representative here immediately? If the GPC couldn't find a plastic surgeon to come in any reasonable period of time, the whole hospital could fold. Every dollar of the GPC's funding, and all the other donations she'd managed to round up, had been spent renovating the nearly destroyed building, buying expensive equipment and hiring all the nurses, techs and other employees needed to run the place. And the money she'd borrowed to build the new wing was already racking up interest charges.

Adrenaline rushed through her veins as she straightened in her seat. The end justified the means. The hospital absolutely could not close and the plastic surgery wing had to open. It had to be there to help all the people who had horrible, disfiguring injuries left from the war. It had to help all the kids living with congenital deformities, like cleft palates, which they'd never have had to live with if they'd been born somewhere else. Somewhere with the kind of healthcare access she was determined to offer.

If the Gilchrist Foundation insisted on sticking with the contract stipulations, she had no choice but somehow to make sure Trent stayed on until the money was in her hand.

CHAPTER SIX

TRENT HAD BEEN relieved that Charlotte wasn't in the hospital commons for dinner. He hadn't wanted to make small talk with her while pretending he didn't feel insulted by her words.

The book he tried to read didn't hold his attention, and he paced in the sparse little bedroom until he couldn't take the confinement anymore. He headed into the humid, oppressive air and strode down the edges of the road, avoiding the muddy ruts as best he could.

When he'd first met Charlotte, he'd been impressed with her enthusiastic commitment to this place, to her vision of what she wanted it to become. And, as they'd spent time together, she'd seemed interested in his life. She'd asked smart and genuine questions, and he'd found himself opening up, just a little—sharing a few stories he usually kept to himself, nearly talking to her about things he just plain didn't talk about.

But, when it came right down to it, she was

like anyone else: a woman who questioned who he was and why he did what he did. Who didn't particularly care what he wanted from his own life. Had she asked him *why* he didn't do plastic surgery exclusively? Expressed any interest in his reasons?

No. She'd just made the same snap judgment others had made. She'd told him what he should do, convinced she knew. Exactly like the woman in his life he'd trusted completely to have his back, to know him, to care.

A trust he'd never give again.

It was disappointing as hell. Then again, maybe this was a good thing. Maybe it would help him feel less drawn to her.

He needed to see this as a positive, not a negative. And, when he left in just a day or two, maybe the peculiar closeness he felt to her would be gone. He'd leave and hope to hell his world would be back to normal.

He kept walking, not having any particular destination in mind, just feeling like he didn't want to go back to that room and smother, but not wanting to chit-chat with people in the hospital either. Maybe he should call up a buddy on the phone, one of the fraternity of mission doctors who understood his life and why he did what he did. They always made him laugh and put any personal troubles in perspective.

As he pulled his cell from his pocket, he noticed a light up ahead. Had he somehow got turned around? He peered through the darkness and realized he was practically at Charlotte's doorstep. Had his damned stupid feet unconsciously brought him here because he'd been thinking of her so intently?

About to turn off on a different path, he was surprised to see little Patience bound out the door, holding a rope with a tiny puppy attached, bringing it down the porch steps. It sniffed around before doing its business, and Trent wanted to laugh at the look of distaste on the little girl's face as she picked up a trowel from the steps.

He didn't want to scare her by appearing out of nowhere in the darkness. "You have a new dog, Patience? When did you get it?"

She looked up at him and smiled. "Hi, Mr. Trent! Yes, Daddy got me another doggie. After my poor Rex was killed by that ugly, wild dog, I been asking and asking. He finally said yes, and my friends at the school like having her to play with too."

"What's its name?"

"Lucky—cos I'm lucky to have her. Except for this part." The look of distaste returned, replacing the excitement as she gripped the trowel. "I promised Daddy I would do everything to take care of her."

He scratched the cute little pup behind the ears, chuckling at the way its entire hind end wagged in happiness before he reached for the trowel. A little doggie doo-doo was nothing compared to many of the things he'd dealt with. "Here. I'll do it for you this time." With a grateful smile, Patience let him dig a hole to bury the stuff. "What are you and your new pup doing here at Charlotte's house?"

"Miss Charlie fixed dinner for me and Daddy. They talking about work."

The door opened and the shadow of John Adams's big body came onto the porch. "Somebody out here with you, Patience?"

"Mr. Trent, Daddy. He's meeting Lucky."

"Trent. Come on inside. Charlie and I were just talking about you."

Damn. He didn't want to know what they were talking about and didn't particularly want to see

Charlotte. But his feet headed up the steps, with Patience and the puppy trailing behind.

The warm glow of the quaint room, full of an odd mix of furniture styles and colorful rugs, embraced him as he stepped inside and he wondered what it was about this old house that gave it so much charm and appeal. An old upright piano against a wall had open sheet music leaning against the stand. Charlotte, dressed in sweatpants and a T-shirt, was curled on a sofa, and she looked up, her lips slightly parted.

The surprise in her green eyes gave way to a peculiar mix of wariness and warmth. As their gazes collided, as he took in the whole of her silken hair and lovely face, he was instantly taken back to earlier today. To their physical closeness beneath that umbrella. To the moment it had felt like it was just the two of them, alone and intimate. Despite all his promises to himself and to her, he'd found himself for that brief second leaning in to taste her mouth, to enjoy the sweetness of her lips.

Being in her house again sent his thoughts to the moment they'd sat on that sofa and kissed until both of them were breathless, ending up making love on the floor. Why did this woman make him feel this way every time he looked at her?

"Trent. I'm…surprised to see you."

Could she be thinking about their time together here too? "I was taking a walk. Then saw Patience and her new pup."

Patience ran to the piano and tapped on the keys, bobbing back and forth as the dog pranced around yapping. "Lucky likes to sing and dance, Mr. Trent, see?"

"She has a beautiful voice." As he smiled at the child, he was struck by a longing to go to the piano himself. To finger the keys as he'd done from the time he was six, until he'd left the U.S. for good. He hadn't realized until he'd first walked into this room with Charlotte a few days ago how much he'd missed playing.

"Miss Charlie has a very pretty voice," Patience enthused. "Please play for us, Miss Charlie. Play and sing something!"

Charlotte shook her head. "Not tonight. I'm sure Mr. Trent doesn't want a concert."

Her cheeks were filled with color. Surely the ultra-confident Charlotte Edwards wasn't feeling shy about performing for him? "Of course I'd like to hear you. What's your favorite thing she plays, Patience?" Surprised at how much he wanted to hear Charlotte sing, he settled himself into a chair, figuring there was no way she could say no to the cute kid.

"That song from church I like: *How Great Thou Art*. Please, Miss Charlie?" The child's hands were clasped together and for once she stood still, her eyes bright and excited.

As Trent had predicted, Charlotte gave a resigned sigh. "All right. But just the one song."

She moved to the piano, and his gaze slid from her thick hair to the curve of her rear, sexy even in sweatpants. Her fingers touched the keyboard, the beginning measures a short prelude to the simple arrangement before she began to sing. Trent forgot about listening to the resonance of the piano's sounding board and heard only the sweet, clear tones of Charlotte's voice, so moving and lovely his chest ached with the pleasure of it.

When the last piano note faded and the room became quiet, he was filled with a powerful desire for the moment to continue. To never end. Without thought, he found himself getting up from the chair to sit next to Charlotte, his hip nudging hers to scoot over on the bench.

"Let's sing a Beatles tune Patience might like,"

he said, his hands poised over the keys, his eyes fixed on the beautiful green of hers. He began to play *Lean On Me* and, when she didn't sing along, bumped his shoulder into hers. "Come on. I know you know it."

"Yes, Miss Charlie! Please sing!" Patience said, pressing her little body against Charlotte's leg.

John Adams began to sing in a slightly off-key baritone before Charlotte's voice joined in, the dulcet sound so pure it took Trent's breath away. When his hands dropped from the keyboard, he looked down into Charlotte's face, seeing Patience next to her, and he was struck with a bizarre and overwhelming vision of a life he hadn't even considered having: a special woman by his side, a family to love; the ultimate utopia.

"That was wonderful," she said, her eyes soft. "I didn't know you could play. Without music, even."

He drew in a breath to banish his disturbing thoughts. "I was shoved onto a piano bench from the time I was little, and had a very intimidating teacher who made sure I was classically trained." He grinned. "I complained like heck sometimes when I had to practice instead of throwing a football around with my friends, but I do enjoy it." He hadn't realized how much until just now, shoulder to shoulder with her, sharing this intimate moment.

"Play something classical. Simple modern songs are about it for my repertoire."

He thought about what he'd still have memorized from long ago and realized it shouldn't be Bach or Haydn. That it should be something romantic, for her. "All right, but don't be surprised if I'm a little rusty. I bet you know this one: Debussy's *Clair de Lune*."

When the last notes of the piece died away, the softness on her face only inches from his had him nearly leaning in for a kiss, forgetting everything but how much he wanted to, and the only thing that stopped him was Patience's little face staring up at him from next to the keyboard.

"I liked that, Mr. Trent!"

"Yes." Charlotte's voice was a near-whisper as she rested her palm on his arm. "That was… beautiful."

As he looked at the little girl, and stared into Charlotte's eyes filled with a deep admiration, the whole scene suddenly morphed from intimate and perfect to scary as hell. Why was he sitting here having fantasies about, almost a longing for, a life he absolutely did not want?

Abruptly, he stood. He needed to get out of there before he said or did something stupid.

Hadn't he, just earlier this evening, been annoyed and disappointed in her? Then one more hour with her and, bam, he was back to square one with all those uncomfortable and mixed feelings churning around inside. What the hell was wrong with him, he didn't want to try to figure out.

"You know, I need to head back to my quarters. I'm going to get most of my things packed up. I'm sure the GPC let you know the new temp is coming in just a day or two?"

"We need to talk about that." The softness that had been in her eyes was replaced by a cool and professional expression. He was damned if it didn't irritate him when he should be glad. "We have an issue."

"What issue?"

She glanced at John Adams before returning her attention to Trent. "Come sit down and we'll talk."

"I'm happy standing, thanks." Her words sounded ominous and he folded his arms across his chest, the disconcerting serenity he'd been feeling just a moment ago fading away like a mirage in the desert. He had a feeling this conversation had something to do with him staying longer, and that wasn't happening.

"The new temp is delayed. I'm not sure when he's going to get here." She licked those tempting lips of hers and, while her expression was neutral, her eyes looked strained and worried. As they should have.

"I told you not to try to guilt me into staying. I can't be here indefinitely." Except, damn it, as he said the words the memory of the comfort he'd felt a moment ago, that sense of belonging, made it sound scarily appealing.

"I'm not trying to guilt you into anything. I'm simply telling you the facts. Which are that, if you leave, there won't be another surgeon here for a while."

"The GPC does a good job finding docs to fill in when there's a gap. Especially when a place has nobody. Besides, you have Thomas here, and he does a great job on the hernias and other simple procedures."

"But what if we get another appendicitis case?

Ectopic pregnancy? Something serious he can't handle?"

He shoved his hands into his pockets and turned to pace across the room, staring out the window at the heavy blackness of the night sky. Looking anywhere but into her pleading eyes.

"If there's one thing I've learned over the years, it's that one person can't save everybody who needs help, Charlotte. I'd be dead if I tried to be that person. Think about the ramifications of this for others, too: the longer I'm here, the more the snowball effect of docs having to fill in where I'm supposed to be next, which is the Philippines." He turned to her, hoping to see she understood what he was saying—not that the idea of staying here longer was both appealing and terrifying. "If the GPC hospital in the Philippines doesn't have anyone because I'm not there, is that okay? Better for patients there to die, instead of patients here?"

Her hands were clasped together so tightly her knuckles were white. "Just a couple of weeks, Trent. Maybe less, if it works out."

He shook his head. "I'm sorry, Charlotte. As soon as my release paperwork comes through from the GPC, I have to head out."

"Trent, all I'm asking is…"

The room that had felt so warm and welcoming now felt claustrophobic. He turned his attention to John Adams so he wouldn't have to look at her wide and worried eyes. "I have a few patients scheduled for surgery early, so I'm going to get to bed. If either of you know of patients needing surgery, you should schedule them in the next couple days before I leave." He scratched the dog behind the ears before he walked out the door, finding it impossible to completely stuff down the conflicting emotions that whirled within him.

As he walked through the darkness, a possible solution struck him that would assuage his guilt. Maybe a phone call to an old friend would solve all his problems and let him move on.

CHAPTER SEVEN

"HOW THE HELL are you, Trent?"

Trent smiled to hear Chase Bowen's voice on the phone. He'd worked with Chase for a number of years in different parts of the world, and the man had been the steadiest, most committed mission doctor he'd ever met. Until a certain wonderful woman had swept into the man's life, their little one in tow, and had changed him into a committed dad rooted in the States.

"I'm good. Decided to try to get hold of you during my lunch break before I see some patients in the clinic this afternoon. How's Drew doing?" When he'd heard the shocking news that Chase and Dani's little boy had cancer, it had scared the crap out of him. Thank goodness they'd caught it in time and the prognosis was excellent.

"He's doing great." The warmth and pride in Chase's voice came through loud and clear. "Completely healthy now, swimming like a fish and growing like crazy. So where are you working?"

"I'm filling in as a temp here in Liberia, hoping to head off on vacation soon, but there are some issues getting a new doc here." A problem he knew Chase was more than familiar with.

"So who's the lucky woman vacationing with you this time? Where are you going?"

"Still figuring all that out." No reason to tell Chase about his weird feelings, that he hadn't been able to find an interest in calling anyone. The man would laugh his butt off, then suggest he see a shrink. "How's Dani?"

"Wonderful. I haven't told you that Drew's going to have a baby brother or sister."

"That's great news. Congratulations." Of all the people he knew, Chase was the last one he'd ever have expected mostly to leave mission work to have a family. But he had to admit, the man seemed happy as hell. "You doing any mission stints at all?"

"Dani and I have gone twice to Honduras together, then I stayed for another week after she headed home. It's worked out well."

"You have any interest in coming to Liberia for just a week or so to fill in for me until the new doc gets here? The GPC needs me to head to the Philippines as soon as possible." Which wasn't exactly true, but he was going with it anyway, damn it.

"I don't know." Chase was silent on the line for a moment. "I'd really like to, but I'm not sure now's a good time. Dani's been a little under the weather, and I wouldn't want to leave her alone with Drew if she's not up to it. Let me talk to her and I'll call you back."

"Great. Give her a hug for me, and tell her I'm happy for both of you. And Drew too."

"Will do. Talk to you soon."

Trent shoved the phone in his pocket and headed back into the hospital. He'd known it was a long shot to think Chase might be able to fill in for him, but with any luck maybe it could still be a win-win. Chase could enjoy a short stint in Africa and Trent could shake the clinging dust of this place off his feet and forget all about Charlotte and her work ethic, spunkiness and warmth.

He thought about Dani, Chase and Drew and their little family that was about to grow. A peculiar sensation filled his chest and he took a moment to wonder what exactly it was. Then he realized with a shock that it was envy.

Envy? Impossible. He'd never wanted that kind of life: a wife who would have expectations of who you should be and how you should live. Kids you were responsible for. A life rooted in one place.

But there was no mistaking that emotion for anything else, and he didn't understand where the hell it had come from. Though Chase had never wanted that kind of life either—until he'd met a woman who had changed how he viewed himself.

The thought set an alarm clanging in his brain. He didn't want to change how he viewed himself. He'd worked hard to be happy with who he was and what he wanted from his life, leaving behind those who hadn't agreed with that view. Now wasn't the time to second-guess all that.

Resolutely shaking off all those disturbing feelings, he continued down the hospital corridor, hoping Charlotte's office door was closed, as it often was, since he had to walk by to get to the clinic. Unfortunately, the door was wide open and her melodic voice drifted into the hallway as she talked with John Adams.

"I'll be fine. I know how to use a gun, remember?"

"I'm not okay with that, Charlie. Patience and I'll pack a bag and move in for a few days until we're sure it was a one-time thing."

A gun? What was a one-time thing? He stopped in the doorway and looked in to see John Adams standing with his arms folded across his chest, a deep frown creasing his brow, and Charlotte staring back with her mulish expression in place.

"Except somebody needs to be at the school too, you know. After all the work and money we've put into the place, we can't risk it being wrecked up and having things stolen."

"What are you talking about?" Trent asked.

"This is not your concern, Trent. John Adams, please close the door so we can talk."

Trent stretched his arm across the door to hold it open. "Uh-uh. You want me to be stuck here for a while longer, you need to include me. What's going on?"

"Somebody broke into her house early this morning after she came to work. When she went there at lunch to get something, she found the door jimmied open and some things gone."

Trent stared at John Adams then swung his gaze to Charlotte. She frowned at him, her lips pressed together, but couldn't hide the tinge of worry in the green depths of her eyes. "What the hell? What was stolen?"

"A radio. The folding chairs I keep in a closet.

Weird stuff. Thankfully, I had my laptop with me at work. It's not a big deal."

"It is a big deal." The protectiveness for her that surged in his veins was sudden and intense. "You can't stay there alone, period. The obvious solution is for John Adams to stay in their quarters at the school, and for me to stay with you until I leave."

Had those words really come out of his mouth? It would be torture to stay in her house with her, knowing she was close by at night in her bed. Bringing back hot memories of their night together. Making him think of the unsettling closeness and connection he'd felt while they'd sat at the piano together singing.

But there was no other option. Keeping her safe was more important than protecting himself from the damned annoying feelings that kept resurfacing.

"That's ridiculous, Trent." Her eyes still looked alarmed, but he was pretty sure it wasn't just about the break-in. "I'll be fine. Whoever it was probably just hit the place once and isn't likely to come back."

"You have no idea if that's true or not." He stepped to her desk and pressed his palms on it, leaning across until his face was as close to hers as hers had been to his at the airport. She smelled so damned good, and the scent of her and the lip gloss she was wearing made him want to find out what flavor gloss it was. "So, you never did tell me," he said, mimicking what she'd said to him at the airport. "What makes you so damned stubborn and resistant to accepting help when you need it? Except when it comes to the hospital, that is?"

"I'm not stubborn. I just don't think this is worth getting all crazy about."

"Maybe not. But it's not a hardship for me to stay at your house so you're not alone until we see if this is a one-time thing or not." So, yeah, that wasn't true. It would be a hardship to be so close to her without taking advantage of it, but no way was he leaving her at risk.

"Good." John Adams spoke from behind him. "Thanks, Trent. I appreciate it. I'm going back to the school now. See you both later."

He straightened. "I've got patients to see in the clinic then I'll get my things. See you back here at six."

"Seriously, Trent—"

"Six."

As he headed to the clinic, he was aware of a ridiculous spring in his step, while at the same time his chest felt a little tight. Obviously, his attraction to Charlotte was keeping the smarter side of his brain from remembering why he needed to keep his distance. And how the hell he was going to keep that firmly in mind while sharing her roof was a question to which he had to find an answer.

"So, Colleen, I'm all set!" Charlie forced a cheerful and upbeat tone to her voice. "Trent has agreed to stay on until the Gilchrist rep does his evaluation. So you can wait to schedule Perry Cantwell until then."

"That's great news for you, Charlie! So all your worries were for nothing."

The warmth in her friend's voice twisted her stomach into a knot. Lying to her felt every bit as bad as lying to Trent, but what choice did she have? "Yes, no worries." Oh, if only that were true.

"I'll let Perry know so he can plan his schedule. After the Gilchrist rep comes, give me a call to tell me how it goes."

"Will do. Thanks, Colleen." Charlie hung up and dropped her head into her hands.

How had her life become a disaster?

As if it wasn't enough to have the bank breathing down her neck, the plastic surgeon indefinitely delayed, Gilchrist insisting on the original stipulations of their agreement and having to skulk around lying to Trent and Colleen, she had a burglar who might come back and a gorgeous man she couldn't stop thinking about spending the night in her bed.

No. Not in her bed. In her spare bedroom. But that was almost as bad. Knowing his long, lean, sexy body was just a few walls away would be tempting, to say the least. But now there was an even better reason to steer clear of getting it on with him again for the days he was here.

She was pretty sure that if he knew she was delaying Perry Cantwell's arrival and had shoved his release papers beneath a pile on her desk he wouldn't take it lightly. In fact, she was more than sure that his easygoing smile would disappear and a side she hadn't seen yet would emerge—a very angry side— and she wouldn't even be able to blame him for it.

Her throat tight, Charlie took inventory of the

new supply delivery, trying not to look at the big invoice that came with it. This whole deception thing felt awful, even more than she'd expected. But she just couldn't see another solution. Thank heavens the Gilchrist Foundation had said their representative should be here within the week. After they gave their approval and she got the check, Trent could be on his way. No harm, no foul, right?

The end justifies the means, she reminded herself again.

With a box of syringes in her arms, she stepped on a stool, struggling to shove the box onto a supply shelf, when a tall body appeared next to her. Long-fingered hands took the box and tucked it in front of another.

"Why don't you just ask for help from someone who's not as vertically challenged as you are?" Trent asked, his eyes amused, grasping her hand as she stepped off the stool.

Looking at his handsome, smiling face so close to hers, a nasty squeeze of guilt made it a little hard to breathe. She didn't even want to think about how that affable expression would change if he knew about her machinations.

"Just because I'm not tall doesn't mean I'm

handicapped. And I'm perfectly capable of getting off a stool by myself."

"I know. I only helped you to see those green eyes of yours flash in annoyance. Amuses me, for some reason."

"Everything amuses you." Except, probably, liars.

"Not true. Burglars don't amuse me. So are we eating here, or at your house to crack heads if anybody shows up?"

His low voice made her stomach feel squishy, even though he was talking about cracking heads. "Nobody's going to show up. And I still don't think you need to come. I have a gun, and I doubt you're very good at cracking heads anyway."

"Don't count on that." The curve of his lips flattened and his eyes looked a little hard. "Anybody tries breaking into your house, you'll find out exactly how good I am."

The thought of exactly how good she knew he was at a number of things left her a little breathless. "I just want to be clear about the ground rules—"

"Dr. Trent." Thomas appeared in the doorway and Charlie put a little distance between her and Trent, not wanting to give the gossip machine any more ammo than they might already have. "There's a boy in the clinic whose mother brought him in because he's not eating. I did a routine exam, but I don't see anything other than a slightly elevated temperature. He is acting a little odd, though, and his mother's sure something's wrong, so I thought you should come take a look."

"Not eating?" Trent's brows lowered. "That's not a very significant complaint. Did you look to see if he has strep or maybe tonsillitis?"

"His throat looks normal to me."

"Hmm. All right." He turned his baby blues to Charlie. "Don't be going home until I come back. I mean it."

"How about if I come along? I haven't had time to visit the clinic for a while." She might not be in medicine, but the way doctors and nurses figured out a diagnosis always fascinated her. And she had to admit she couldn't resist the chance to watch Trent in action again.

"Of course, Ma," Thomas said, turning to lead the way.

CHAPTER EIGHT

THE BOY, WHO looked to be about ten years old, was sitting on the exam table with a peculiar expression on his face, as though he was in pain. "Hey, buddy," Trent said, giving him a reassuring smile. "Your mommy tells us you're having trouble eating. Does your stomach hurt?"

The child shook his head without speaking. Checking his pulse, Trent noted that he was sweaty, then got a tiny whiff of an unpleasant odor. It could be just that the child smelled bad, or it could be a symptom of some infection.

"Let's take a look in your throat." Using a tongue depressor, he studied the boy's mouth, but didn't see any sign of an abscess or a bad tooth. No tonsil problem or strep. Once Trent was satisfied that none of those were the problem, the boy suddenly bit down on the stick and kept it clamped between his teeth. "Okay, I'm done looking in your mouth. Let go of the stick, please."

The boy didn't budge, then started to cry without opening his mouth. Trent gently pressed his thumb and fingers to the boy's jaw to encourage him to relax and unclamp his jaw. "Let me take the stick out now and we'll check some other things." The boy kept crying and it was all Trent could do to get him to open his mouth barely wide enough to remove the stick.

Damn. Trent thought of one of his professors long ago talking about giving the spatula test, and that sure seemed to be what had just happened with the stick. "Did you hurt yourself any time the past week or two? Did something poke into your skin?"

"I'nt know." The words were a mumble, the boy barely moving his lips, and Trent was now pretty sure he knew what was wrong.

"Thomas, can you get me a cup of water?"

"Yes, doctor."

When he returned with the cup, Trent held it to the boy's lips. "Take a sip of this for me, will you?" As he expected, the poor kid gagged on the water, unable to swallow.

"All right. I want you to lie down so I can check a few things." Trent tried to help him lie on the exam table, but it was difficult with the child's body so rigid. The simple movement sent the boy into severe muscle spasms. When the spasms eventually faded and Trent finally was able to get him prone, the child's arms flung up to hug his chest tightly while his legs stayed stiff and straight. He began crying again, his expression formed into a grimace.

Trent was aware of both Thomas and Charlotte standing by the table, staring with surprise and concern. He grasped the boy's wrist and tried to move his elbow. The arm resisted, pushing against his hand.

"What do you think is wrong, Trent?" Charlotte said, obviously alarmed.

He couldn't blame her for being unnerved, since this wasn't something you saw every day. It was damned disturbing how a patient was affected by this condition.

"Tetanus. I'm willing to bet he's had a puncture wound, probably in the foot, that maybe he didn't even notice happened. The infection, wherever it is, is causing his jaw to lock, as well as all the other symptoms we're seeing."

He released the child's arm and lifted his foot, noting it was slightly swollen. Bingo! There it was: a tiny wound oozing a small amount of smelly pus.

The poor kid was still crying, the sound pretty horrible through his clenched teeth. He placed the boy's foot back down and refocused his attention on calming him down. "You're going to be all right, I promise. I know this is scary and you feel very uncomfortable and strange. But I'm going to get rid of the infection in your foot and give you medicine to make you feel better. Okay?"

The brown eyes that stared back at him were terrified, and who could blame the poor little guy? With tetanus, painful spasms could be so severe they actually pulled ligaments apart or broke bones.

"What do you do for tetanus?" Charlotte asked. "Is it…?" She didn't finish the sentence, but he knew what she was asking.

"He'll recover fine, now that we've got him here. Thomas, can you get what we need for an IV drip of penicillin? And some valium, please."

"Penicillin?" Charlotte frowned and leaned up to speak softly in his ear. "Since he's so sick, shouldn't you give him something—I don't know—stronger?"

"Maybe it's a good thing you're not a doctor

after all." He couldn't resist teasing her a little. "In the U.S., they'd probably use an antibiotic that costs four hundred dollars a day and kills practically every bacteria in your body instead of just the one causing the disease—kind of like killing an ant with a sledgehammer. But, believe me, penicillin is perfect for this. You can't kill bacteria deader than dead."

Her pretty lips and eyes smiled at him. "Okay. I believe you. So that's it? Penicillin? Do you need a test to confirm that's what it is?"

"No, his symptoms are clear. That's what it is." He found himself feeling pleased that she trusted him to make the right decision. Since when had he ever needed other people to appreciate what he did and what he'd learned over the years?

He reached to pat the child's stiffly folded arms. "Hang in there. I'll be right back." Grasping Charlotte's elbow, he walked far enough away that the boy couldn't hear them.

"Penicillin is just part of the treatment. We'll need to do complete support care. I have to get rid of the clostridium tetani, which is the bacteria in his foot that's giving off the toxin to the rest of his body. It's one of the most lethal toxins on earth, which is why it's a damned good thing his mother brought him in. He wouldn't have made it if it was left untreated."

She shuddered. "How do you get rid of the… whatever it was called…tetani toxin?"

"I'll have to open his foot to remove it and clean out the dead and devitalized tissue so it can heal. It'll give the penicillin a chance to work. I'll give him fluids and valium to keep him comfortable so he can rest. He'll have to stay here several days, kept very quiet, to give his body time to process the toxin."

She nodded and her eyes smiled at him again, her soft hand wrapping around his forearm. "Thank you again for coming back, Trent. I bet our lying Dr. Smith would never have been able to figure out what was wrong with this boy. You're…amazing."

He didn't know about all that. What he did know was that *she* was amazing. In here, looking at this boy, concerned and worried but not at all freaked out by the bizarre presentation of tetanus, despite not being in medicine herself. He'd bet a whole lot of his fortune that the women he'd dated back in the days of his old, privileged life in the States would have run hysterically from the room. Or, even more likely, would never been in there to begin with.

"I have to take care of his foot right now, which is going to take a little time. Promise you'll stay here in the hospital until I'm done?" He found himself reaching to touch her face, to stroke his knuckles against her cheek. "I know you think you're all tough and can handle any big, bad burglar that might be ransacking your house as you walk in the door. But, for my peace of mind, will you please wait for me?"

"I'll wait for you." The beautiful green of her eyes, her small smile, her words, all seemed to settle inside his chest and expand it. "Since it'll be past time for dinner to be served here, I'll fix something for us when we get there."

"Sounds great." He wanted to lean down and kiss her, the way he had in the rain the other day. And the reasons for not doing that began to seem less and less important. Charlotte definitely didn't act like she'd be doing much pining after he was gone.

That was good news he hoped was really true, and the smart part of him knew it was best to keep it that way, to keep their relationship "strictly professional," and never mind that he'd be spending the night back in her house. The house in which, when the two of them *weren't* just colleagues, they hadn't gotten much sleep at all.

Despite the comfort of the double bed, with its wrought-iron headboard and soft, handmade quilt, Trent turned restlessly, finally flopping onto his back with his hands behind his head. The room was girly, with lace curtains, a pastel hooked rug and an odd mix of furniture. The femininity of it made him even more acutely aware that Charlotte was sleeping very close by.

Every time he closed his eyes, he saw her face: the woman who had fascinated him from the first second he'd walked into her office. That long, silky brown hair cascading down her back, her body with curves in all the right places on her petite frame and her full lips begging to be kissed were as ultra-feminine as the bedroom.

But her willful, no-nonsense personality proved that a woman who oozed sexiness and femininity sure didn't have to be quiet and docile.

He'd guessed being here would be a challenge. How the hell was he going to get through the night keeping his word that their relationship would stay strictly professional? Get through the next few days?

Focusing on work seemed like a good plan. He'd tell her he wanted to head into the field to do immunizations, or whatever else patients might need, keeping close proximity to Charlotte at a minimum. The last thing he wanted to do was hurt her, and so far it seemed their brief time together hadn't negatively affected her at all. No point in risking it—not to mention that he didn't want to stir up that strange discomfort he'd felt at the airport when he'd tried to get out of there the first time.

A loud creak sent Trent sitting upright in bed, on high alert. Had someone broken in? Surely, lying there wide awake, he would have heard other sounds if that was the case?

Probably Charlotte wasn't sleeping well, either. He stared at the bedroom door, his pulse kicking up a notch at another creak that sounded like it was coming from the hall. Could she possibly be planning to come into his room?

He swung his legs to the floor and sat there for a few minutes, his ears straining to hear if it was her, or if he should get up to see if what he'd heard was an intruder. While it seemed unlikely someone could break in without making a lot of noise, he threw on his khaki shorts and decided he had to check the place out just to be sure.

He opened the bedroom door as quietly as possible and crept out in his bare feet, staring through the darkness of the hallway, looking for any movement. The scent of coffee touched his nose and he relaxed, since he was pretty sure no intruder would be taking a coffee break.

Charlotte was up; he should just go back to bed. But, before he knew what he was doing, he found himself padding down the narrow staircase to the kitchen.

"Did you have to make so much racket in here? I was sound asleep," he lied as he stepped into the cozy room. Seeing Charlotte standing at the counter in a thin, pink robe, her hair messy, her lips parted in surprise, almost obliterated his resolve to keep his distance. Nearly had him striding across the room to pull her into his arms, and to hell with all his resolutions to the contrary. But he forced himself to lean against the doorjamb and shove his hands in his pockets.

"I was quiet as a mouse. Your guilty conscience must be keeping you awake."

"Except for that 'murdering my old girlfriend'

thing, my conscience is clean. I abandoned my vacation plans, didn't I? Came back here to work for you?"

She nodded and the way her gaze hovered on his bare chest for a moment reminded him why he hadn't been able to sleep, damn it.

"You did," she said, turning back to the percolator. "I'm grateful, and I know Lionel's family is grateful too. And the other patients you've taken care of since then." She reached into the cupboard to grab mugs. "Coffee?"

He should go back upstairs. Try to sleep. "Sure."

He settled into a chair at the table and she joined him, sliding his cup across the worn wood. His gaze slipped to the open vee of her robe. He looked at her smooth skin and hint of the lush breasts he knew were hidden there, pictured what kind of silky nightgown she might be wearing and quickly grabbed up his cup to take a swig, the burn of it on his tongue a welcome distraction.

Time for mundane conversation. "So, tell me about what you studied in school. Didn't you say you got an MBA?"

"Yes. I got a hospital administration degree,

then went to Georgetown for my masters. I knew I'd be coming here to get the hospital open and running again, so all that was good." She leaned closer, her eyes alight with enthusiasm. "I met a lot of people who shared their experiences with me—about how they'd improved existing facilities or started from scratch in various countries. I learned so much, hearing the things they felt they did right or would do differently."

He, too, leaned closer, wanting to study her, wanting to know what made this fascinating and complex woman tick. "I've been surprised more than once how much you know about medicine. Tell me again, why didn't you become a doctor?"

"Somebody needs to run this place. Create new ways to help people, to make a difference. Like I said before, I can get doctors and nurses and trained techs. I focused my training on how to do the rest of it. My parents encouraged that; they've trusted me and John Adams with the job of bringing this place back."

A surge of old and buried pain rose within him and he firmly shoved it back down. It must be nice to have someone in your life who believed in you, who cared what you wanted. It must be nice to have someone in your life who didn't say one thing, all the while betraying you, betraying your blind trust, with a deep stab in your back.

"I've worked at a lot of hospitals in the world. That experience might come in handy if you have any questions."

"Thanks. I might take you up on that."

Her beautiful eyes shone, her mouth curved in a pleased smile, and the urge to grab her up and kiss her breathless was nearly irresistible. Abruptly, he stood and downed the last of his coffee, knowing that between the caffeine and her close proximity there'd be no sleep for him tonight.

"I'm going to hit the hay. Try not to make a bunch of noise again and wake me up. I don't want to fall asleep in the middle of a surgery tomorrow."

She stood too and the twist of her lips told him she knew exactly why he was awake. "Don't worry. The last thing I want to do is disturb your sleep."

"Liar." He had to smile, enjoying the pink that stained her cheeks at the word. "Anyway, you've already done that, so you owe me. Maybe you should disturb my sleep for a few more hours; help me relax."

Why did his mouth say one thing, when his brain told him to shut up and walk out? Until the slow blink of her eyes, the tip of her tongue licking her lips, the rise and fall of that tantalizing vee of skin beneath her robe, obliterated all regrets.

"I don't think your sleep is my responsibility," she said. "You're on your own."

She swayed closer, lids low, her lips parted, practically willing him to kiss her. What was the reason he'd been trying not to? Right now, he couldn't quite remember. Didn't want to.

"Seems to me we agreed you were in charge of my life while I'm here." Almost of their own accord, his feet brought him nearly flush with her body. Close enough to feel her warmth touch his bare chest; to feel her breath feather across his skin. "Got any ideas on a cure for insomnia?"

"Less coffee in the middle of the night? Maybe a hammer to the head? I've got one in the toolbox in the closet."

He reached for her and put his hands on her waist. "I know you said you couldn't promise not to hurt me, but that seems a little drastic." His head lowered because he had to feel her skin against his lips. He touched them softly to her cheek, beneath her ear. "Any other ideas?"

Her warm hands flattened against his chest. When they didn't push, he drew her close, her curves perfectly fitted to his body. Much as he knew he should back off right now, there was no way he could do it. He wanted her even more than the night they'd fallen into her bed together. And that night had knocked him flat in a way he couldn't remember ever having experienced before.

Her head tipped back as he moved his mouth to the hollow of her throat and could feel her pulse hammering beneath his lips. "We have morphine in the drug cupboard at the hospital," she said, her voice breathy, sexy. "A big dose of that might help."

"You're a much more powerful drug than morphine, much more addictive, and you know it." Her green eyes filled his vision before he lowered his mouth to hers and kissed her. He drew her warm tongue into his mouth, and the taste of her robbed him of any thoughts of taking it slow. Of kissing her then backing off.

Her hands roamed over his chest, sending heat racing across his flesh, and he sank deeper into the kiss, tasting the hint of coffee, cream and sweet sugar on his tongue. Her fingers continued on a shivery path down his ribs, to his sides and back, and he wrapped his arms around her and pulled her close, the swell of her breasts rising and falling against him.

His thigh nudged between her legs and, as she rocked against him, he let one hand drift to her rear, increasing the pressure, loving the gasp that left her mouth and swirled into his.

The rattling sound of a doorknob cut through the sensual fog in his brain and Trent pulled his mouth from Charlotte's. They stared at one another, little panting breaths between them, before her gaze cut toward the living room.

"What the hell? Are you expecting someone?"

Her eyes widened and she pulled away from him. "No," she whispered. "Darn, I left my gun upstairs. I'll have to go through the living room to get it. Should I run up there? If he—or they—get in you could punch them or something till I get back down with it. Or maybe you shouldn't. Maybe *they* have a gun."

Metal scratched against metal then a creaking sound indicated the door had been opened, and Charlotte's hands flung to her chest as she stared out of the kitchen then swung her gaze back to Trent.

"The door was locked, wasn't it? Does someone have a key?" It hadn't sounded like forced entry to him. Maybe it was somebody she knew. And the thought that it could be a boyfriend twisted his gut in a way it shouldn't twist for a sweet but short interlude.

"No. The only other key is in my office at the hospital."

Her whisper grew louder, likely because she was afraid. He touched his finger to her lips and lowered his mouth to her ear. "Is there really a hammer in the closet?"

She nodded and silently padded to it in her bare feet, wincing as the door shuddered open creakily. She grabbed the head of a hammer and handed it to him, then pulled out a heavy wrench and lifted it in the air, ready to follow him.

What would she have done if he hadn't been here with her tonight? The thought brought a surge of the same protective anger he'd felt when he'd heard about the first break-in, which had made him more than ready to bust some-body's head.

"Stay here," he whispered. He slipped to the doorway and could see a shadowy figure with a bag standing near the base of the stairs.

CHAPTER NINE

HEART POUNDING, CHARLIE stepped close behind Trent, peeking around him as he stood poised to strike the intruder. Never would she have thought that the burglars would come back, especially at night when she was home. Thank goodness Trent was here. Much as she said she could look after herself—and she could; she was sure she could—having a big, strong man in the house definitely made her glad she wasn't alone as someone was breaking in.

She looked up to see Trent's jaw was taut, his eyes narrowed, his biceps flexed as he raised the hammer. He looked down at her, gave a quick nod, then burst across the room with a speed sure to surprise and overwhelm whoever had broken in.

The man was shorter than Trent, who slammed his shoulder into the intruder's chest like he was an American football linebacker. The intruder landed hard, flat on his back, and Trent stepped over him, one leg on either side of the man's prone figure. With one hand curled in a menacing fist, Trent's other held the hammer high.

"Who the hell are you? And you better answer fast before you can't answer at all," Trent growled.

"What the heck? Who are *you*? Charlie?" Her father's voice sounded scared and trembly and she tore across the room in a rush.

"Oh, heavens! Stop, Trent! It's okay. It's my dad." The wrench in her hand suddenly seemed to weigh twenty pounds and she nearly dropped it as she shook all over in shock and relief. She fell to her knees next to her father, placing the wrench on the floor so she could touch his chest and arms. "Dad, are you all right? Are you hurt?"

"I…I'm not sure." He stared up at Trent, who stepped off him to one side and lowered the hammer. "Next time I'll know to knock, seeing as you have a bodyguard."

"Sorry, sir." Trent crouched down and slipped his arm beneath her dad's shoulders, helping him to a sitting position. "You okay?"

"I think so. Except for the hell of a bruise I'm going to have in the morning." He stood with the help of Trent and Charlie and rubbed his hand across his chest, then offered it to Trent. "I'm Joseph Edwards. Thanks for looking out for my daughter."

"Uh, you're welcome. I guess. Though I think this is the first time I've been thanked for beating somebody up. I'm Trent Dalton."

Charlie glanced at Trent to see that charming, lopsided smile of his as he shook her dad's hand. The shock of it all, and the worry of whether her dad was okay or not, had worn off and left her with a hot annoyance throbbing in her head. "What are you doing here, Dad? I thought you weren't coming for a couple more nights. Why didn't you call? You're lucky you don't have a big lump on your head. Or a gunshot through your chest."

"I tried to call but couldn't get any cell service. After I met with Bob in Monrovia, I decided not to stay at his house like I'd planned, because his wife's not feeling well. Then I got the key from the hospital so I wouldn't wake you—though that obviously wasn't a problem." He raised his eyebrows. "I won't ask what you're doing up in the middle of the night."

"That wouldn't be any of your business," Charlie said, glaring at Trent as his smile grew wider. His grin definitely implied something it shouldn't, and it sure didn't help that the man had no shirt on. Though, as she thought back to what exactly they were doing when her dad had arrived, it wasn't too far off. It had, in fact, been quickly heading in the direction of hot and sweaty sex and she felt her cheeks warm. "But if you must know, Trent is doing surgeries at the hospital for a few days and, um, needed a place to stay. We were just talking about the hospital and stuff."

"She obviously doesn't want you to know, but that's not entirely the truth," Trent said.

She stared at him. Surely the man wasn't going to share the details of their relationship—or whatever you'd call their memorable night together—to her *father?*

"What is the truth?" her dad asked.

"The reason I'm spending the night here is because someone broke into the house yesterday. I didn't think she should be alone until it seemed unlikely the guy was coming back. Which is why I knocked you down first and asked questions later."

"Ah." Her father frowned. "I have to say, it's concerned me from the start that you were living here by yourself. Maybe we should rethink that—have a few hospital employees live here with you."

"I've been here two years, Dad, and nothing like this has happened before. I'm sure it's an isolated incident. I like living alone and don't want that to change."

"Maybe you should get a dog, then—one with a big, loud bark that would scare somebody off."

A dog? Hmm. It might be nice to have a dog around and she had to admit she might feel a touch safer. "If it will ease your mind, I'll consider it."

"We'll talk more about this later." Her dad lowered himself into a chair and rubbed his chest again, poor man. Though she felt he'd brought it on himself by sneaking in. "I'm looking forward to hearing about how the new wing is coming along. Must be about finished, isn't it? When is the first plastic surgeon supposed to get here?"

"Um, soon." She glanced at Trent and saw his brows twitch together. This was her chance to ask him to stay until the Gilchrist rep got here, to do a few plastic surgery procedures, since the subject had come up. Maybe, with her dad there, he wouldn't be so quick to say no. She pulled the ties of her robe closer together, trying not to give off any vibes that said, *I'm desperate here.*

"Trent. Ever since I saw what a wonderful job you did on Lionel's eye, I've been meaning to ask." She licked her lips and forged on. "There are a few patients who've been waiting a long time to have a plastic surgery procedure done. Would you consider doing one or two before you leave?"

"You know, I'm not actually a board-certified plastic surgeon." His eyes were unusually flat and emotionless. "Better for you to wait until you have your whole setup ready and a permanent surgeon in place."

"You do plastic surgery?" Her father's eyebrows lifted in surprise. "I assumed you were a general surgeon, like the ones who usually rotate through the GPC-staffed hospitals."

"I am."

"Come on, Trent." Charlie tried for a cajoling tone that might soften him up. "I saw what you did for Lionel's eye. You told me, when you wanted to do it, that I didn't know who I was dealing with, remember? And you were right."

He looked at her silently for a moment before he spoke. "I'm leaving here any day now, Charlotte. It wouldn't make sense for me to perform any complex plastics procedures on patients, then take off before I could follow up with them."

"Please, Trent." Her hands grew cold. "Maybe you could even stay a few extra days, to help these patients who so desperately need it. When you see some of them, I think you'll want to."

"I can't stay longer. And it's not good medical practice for me to do a surgery like that, then leave. I'm sorry." He turned to her dad, the conversation clearly over by the tone of his voice. "Since you're here tonight, sir, I'm going to grab my things and head back to my quarters."

Charlie watched him disappear up the steps and listened to his footsteps fade away down the hall. Why was he so adamant about this? And what could she possibly do to convince him?

Trent managed to avoid Charlotte the entire following day. He took dinner to his room, and if she noticed she didn't say anything. When his phone rang and he saw it was Chase, a strange feeling came over him before he answered. A feeling that told him he'd miss this place when he left, whether it was tomorrow or days from now.

"So, I'm sorry, man, but it's just not going to

work out," Chase said in his ear. "Wish I could sub for you. I'd love to head back to Africa for a week or so. But I'm pretty busy at work here and, like I said, Dani's not feeling great this month. Says she didn't have morning sickness with Drew, but she sure does now."

"Maybe it's you that's making her sick this time, and not her pregnancy," Trent said. "Which I could fully appreciate."

"Yeah, that could well be true." Chase chuckled. "Any chance you'll be coming to the States some time? Dani and I go to the occasional conference here. It would be great to catch up."

"No plans for that right now. I'll let you know if I do." He wouldn't mind a visit back to the States, so long as it wasn't New York City. It would be nice to see Chase and Dani, and maybe even cute little Drew and his new baby sibling. He hadn't been back for quite a while. "Who knows, maybe we can temp at the same time in Honduras when I'm between jobs. Let's see if we can make that happen."

"That would be great. Stay in touch, will you?

"Will do. Take care, and give your family a hug for me."

Well, damn. He shoved his phone in his pocket.

So much for that great idea. But he'd known it was a long shot that Chase would be able to fill in for him here in Liberia until the new doctor arrived.

The uneasy feelings he had about being stuck here were peculiar and annoying. It wasn't like it was a big deal if he went on his vacation all by his lonesome tomorrow or a couple weeks from now. The GPC was used to delays like this, so they probably had a temp lined up for him in the Philippines until he got there.

But this tug and push he kept feeling around Charlotte was damned uncomfortable. One minute all he wanted was to kiss her breathless, knowing that was a bad idea for all kinds of reasons; the next, she was bugging him about doing plastic surgery that he plain didn't want to do, which put the distance between them he knew they should keep in place. That he knew he should welcome.

There had been a number of times his plastics skills had come in handy over the years, doing surgeries on a cleft palate, or a hemangioma like Lionel's, that were important to how the patient could function every day. But actually working in a plastic surgery hospital? One dedicated to procedures that mostly improve someone's looks? No, thank you. He'd rather keep people alive than just make them look better to the world.

He sat at the tiny desk in his room and went through the mail that had arrived this week. One was from the GPC and he tore it open, wondering if it was finally his release papers, or if they'd had to relocate his next job to somewhere other than the Philippines because of this delay.

Perplexed, he read through the letter twice. Clearly, there was some mess-up here. How come the director, Mike Hardy, thought the new doctor was already at the Edwards Hospital? Mike's letter advised him that, because of the imminent arrival of this doctor in Liberia, a temp filling in at his new job wouldn't be necessary and he could still take his full three weeks off. His revised arrival date in the Philippines was exactly three weeks from today.

He picked up his phone to call Mike, but figured it would make sense to talk to Charlotte first. Maybe she knew something he didn't.

He left his room and strode down the long hallway from the residence quarters into the hospital. Dinner had been over an hour ago, so she very well might be back at home. And he wasn't about to follow her over there. If she'd already left, he'd forget about talking to her and just call Mike.

A glance in her office showed she wasn't there, so he went to the dining hall. Her round, sexy rear was the only part of her he could see. With her head and torso inside a cupboard as she kneeled on the floor, he stopped to enjoy the view and had to resist the urge to shock her by going over and giving that sexy bottom of hers a playful spank.

"Does anyone know if the rest of Charlotte Edwards is in here?" he asked instead.

Her body unfolded and she straightened to look at him, still on her knees. "Very funny. I'm just trying to organize this kitchen equipment. Too many cooks in here are making it hard to find anything when you want it."

"When you have a minute, I need to talk to you about the new doc coming."

He had to wonder why her expression was instantly alarmed. Was she worried there'd been an even longer delay? Thank goodness her dad was here now, so Trent wouldn't be spending any more tempting nights in her house.

She shoved to her feet and walked over. "What about the new doc?"

"I got a letter from Mike Hardy telling me all

systems are go for my vacation. I'm wondering what the mix-up is. Or if someone is coming tomorrow and they somehow forgot to send my release papers."

She snatched the letter from his hand and looked it over, her fingers gripping it until they were practically white. "Um, I don't know. This is weird. Last I heard, there was nobody in place yet. Let me see what I can find out and I'll let you know. Believe me, I'm as anxious to get you out of here as you are to leave."

"Never mind." He tried to tug the paper from her hand, but she held on tight. It pissed him off that she wanted him out of there so badly, which was absolutely absurd, since he wanted the same thing. "I'll call Mike in the morning. Give me my letter back."

"I'm the director of this hospital and staffing is my responsibility."

Her green eyes were flashing irritation at him, as well as something else he couldn't figure out. The woman was like a pit bull sometimes. "Why are you so controlling? Technically, the GPC employs me, you know. And this is my job, my vacation and my life. Give me my letter."

"Fine. Take the letter." She let it go and spun

on her heel toward the doorway. "But I'm going home, then calling Mike. I'm asking you to let me handle this; I'll let you know what he says. Hopefully this means you're on your way very soon."

His hand crumpled the letter slightly as he watched her disappear into the hall. Why he wanted to storm after her and kiss her until she begged him to stay was something he wasn't going to try to understand.

CHAPTER TEN

CHARLIE HELD TRENT'S release papers in slightly shaky hands then shoved them deeper under the pile on her desk. She tried to draw a calming breath and remind herself that Colleen believed Trent had agreed to stay, so the new doctor wouldn't just show up on the doorstep and give Trent the green light to leave. But if Trent called Mike Hardy, who knew what would happen?

She prayed the Gilchrist representative would show up fast. Surely they'd be impressed with what a great job the hospital's plastic surgeon had done on Lionel's eye; they would never know the talented man would be out of there as soon as the rep left. Trent would charm them, even if he didn't know he was supposed to, because the man oozed charm just by breathing. And all would be well. It would.

Paying bills wasn't exactly the way to forget about the problem, but it had to be done. Charlie tore open the mail and grimly dropped every invoice into the box she kept for them. One thing she could do to relieve the stress of it all was work harder on other sources of funding besides Gilchrist. Her dad had always told her to never put all her eggs in one basket, so she tried to have multiple fundraising efforts going. Time to make some more calls and send more letters to previous donors. There was no way any of them would come close to what the Gilchrist Foundation had committed, but something was a whole lot better than nothing.

A letter with a postmark from New York City and the name of some financial organization caught her eye and made her heart accelerate. The Gilchrist Foundation was based in NYC. Could they possibly just have decided to send a check without worrying about the final approval?

She quickly ripped it open then sighed when she read the letterhead: not from the foundation. But her brief disappointment faded as she read the check that was enclosed with the letter. She stared, not quite believing what she was seeing.

Fifty thousand dollars, written to The Louisa Edwards Education Project. With slightly shaky hands, she scanned the letter that came with the check.

*Please find enclosed an anonymous dona-
tion to provide supplemental funding for the
Louisa Edwards School.*

It was signed by someone who apparently worked at the financial firm it came from.

She stared at the bold numerals and the cursive below them. Fifty thousand dollars. Fifty thousand! Oh, heavens!

She leaped up and tore out the door of her office, about to run all the way to the school to show John Adams and her dad, who was there with him. To have John Adams plan to hire another new teacher. To think of all the supplies on their wish-list they'd decided not to buy for now.

And she ran, *kapow*, right into Trent Dalton's hard shoulder, just as she had before when he'd asked if she was late to lunch.

He grabbed her arms to steady her. "Wow, you must be extra-hungry today. Something special on the menu?"

"Funny." She clutched the check to her chest and smiled up at him. "But even you can't annoy me today. You won't believe what just came in the mail!"

"A new designer handbag? Some four-inch

heels?" he asked, little creases at the corners of his eyes as he smiled.

"Way, way better. Guess again."

"A brand-new SUV?"

She held the check up in front of his face. "Look." She was so thrilled she had to gulp in air to keep from hyperventilating. "Somebody sent a check—a huge check—to the school. I have no idea who it's from, or how they even heard about us. We can serve so many more kids now. Get stuff we've been wanting, but couldn't afford. Can you believe it?"

"No. Can't believe it."

There was a funny expression on his face, a little amused smile along with something else she couldn't quite figure out. "You're laughing at me, aren't you? I can't help being excited. More than excited! Oh my gosh, this is so amazing and wonderful. Just like a gift from the heavens."

Beyond jubilant, she flung her arms around Trent's neck and gave him a big, smacking kiss on the lips, because she just plain couldn't help herself. She drew back slightly against his arms, which had slipped across her back, and could see his eyes had grown a tad more serious. The warm kiss he gently pressed to her forehead felt soft and sweet.

"I'm happy for you. You and John Adams deserve it for the work you're accomplishing in that school, and obviously your donor knows that. You're literally changing those kids' lives, giving them a fighting chance in the tough world they live in."

"Thank you. But you change lives too, you know." She stepped out of his hold, instantly missing the warm feel of his arms around her. "Gotta go. I need to tell John Adams and Dad about this."

"I'll come, too. I'm not busy right now and I'd like to see the kids again."

It hadn't rained in a few days, so the earth wasn't nearly as muddy as the last time they'd trekked over to the school. Her brain was spinning with possibilities, until a thought made her excitement drop a notch.

Maybe she shouldn't be so quick to hire another teacher or two and immediately spend some of it on teaching supplies and another couple sewing machines for the students to learn that skill on. Maybe she needed to hold onto it just in case she couldn't pay the hospital bills when they came in if the Gilchrist funding didn't come through.

No. They'd always run the hospital and the school separately: different sponsors and donors, different bookkeeping, different projects. Whoever had donated this money wanted it to go to the school and she had to honor that. It was the only fair and right thing to do for both the donor and the students.

"Did you get hold of Mike about my letter? Or am I allowed to call him now, Miss 'I'm The Director Of The Hospital And The Whole World'?" His lips were curved in a teasing smile, but his eyes weren't smiling quite as much.

"I'm…sorry if I was being bossy and…and acted like I want you to leave. I don't, really. I've just got a lot on my mind." And, boy, wasn't that the truth. "I spoke with Colleen, and apparently she does have someone lined up to come soon, but not today or tomorrow. I'm sorry about that also. I would greatly appreciate it, though, if you would stay just another few days." And all that was the truth, too, which made her feel a tad better. She wasn't being quite as deceitful as she felt.

"All right. Thanks for checking. I guess I can hang around for just a little while longer."

She drew a deep breath of relief, then glanced up at Trent's profile, at his prominent nose, black hair and sensual lips. It didn't feel like just over a week since he'd returned from the airport. As he walked next to her, not touching but close enough to feel his warmth, it seemed much longer. Oddly natural, like she should just reach over to hold his hand.

Which was not good. Not only would he be leaving in a matter of days, she didn't want to think about how shocked and angry he'd be if he ever found out about her little fibs. Okay, big fibs; the thought of it made her stomach knot.

Three figures, two taller and one small, along with a little dog, appeared up ahead on the road—obviously, her dad, John Adams, Patience and Lucky. Seeing them obliterated all other thoughts as Charlie ran the distance between them, waving the check.

"You're going to faint when you see this!"

Trent followed slowly behind Charlotte, not wanting to intrude on her moment, sharing her excitement with the two men and Patience. Though he'd been itching to leave, to move on with his life, he felt glad—blessed, really—that he'd still been here when she got the check. He'd never been around when someone received one of his donations, and it felt great to see how happy it made her. To know it would help them achieve their important goals.

He watched her fling her arms around both men, first her dad, then John Adams, just as she'd done with him. Well, not exactly the same. Her arms wrapped around their middles in a quick hug. That was different from the way she'd thrown her arms around his own neck, drawing his head close, giving him that kiss; her breasts pressing softly against his chest, staying there a long moment, her fingers tucked into his hair, sending a shiver along his scalp and a desire to kiss more than just her forehead.

"You don't know who the donor is?" her father asked.

She shook her head, the sun touching her shining hair as it slipped across her shoulders. "No. I wish I did. I wish I could thank them. That *we* could thank them. Think there's any way to find out?"

"Not likely. But you could always contact the company it came from and ask."

"I'll do that," Charlotte said as they turned and

headed back toward the hospital. "Maybe even ask if there's anything specific they want the money used for."

Trent knew his finance man was discreet and they'd get no information that could trace it back to him. "Whoever donated it stayed anonymous because they wanted to. I say just spend the money as you see fit and know they trusted you to do that," he said.

"Good point, Trent," John Adams said. "We do get the occasional anonymous donation, though nothing like this, of course. I think we should respect that's how they wanted to keep it."

"Okay." Charlotte's chest rose and fell in a deep breath, and Trent found his attention gravitating to her beautiful curves. "I'm feeling less freaked out. Just plain happy now. Why are you three leaving the school?"

"Daddy promised he would take me to the beach," Patience said. "He's been promising and promising, but kept saying it was s'posed to rain. But today the sun is shiny so we can go!" The little girl danced from one foot to the other, the colorful cloth bag on her shoulder dancing along with her.

"Mind if I come?" Trent asked. "I'll build a

sandcastle with you." The kid was so cute, and he hadn't seen an inch of Liberia other than the airport and the road to and from the hospital and school. One of the things he enjoyed about his job was exploring new places, discovering new things. He turned to Charlotte. "Would that be okay? Thomas is taking care of a man needing hernia surgery, and I've already seen the patients in the clinic. The nurses are finishing up with all of them. I can check on everyone when I get back."

"Of course, that's fine. I'll see what's in the kitchen for you all to take for a beach lunch."

"Why don't you go along, Charlie?" her dad suggested. "You never take much time off to do something fun. I've been wanting to go through the information you gave me, anyway, so I can keep an eye on things while you're gone."

"Well…" Her green eyes held some expression he couldn't figure out. Wariness? Anxiety? "I'm not really a beach person, you know. And I don't want you stuck here doing my work, Dad."

"You may be the director, but I'm still a part of this hospital too, remember." Joseph smiled. "You need to get over this fear of yours. Go get your things together. John Adams and I will scrounge up some food for you all to take."

"What fear of yours?" Trent asked. From being around Charlotte just the past week or so, he couldn't imagine her being afraid of much of anything.

"Nothing. Dad's exaggerating."

"Exaggerating? The last time we were at the beach, I thought you were going to hyperventilate just going into the water up to your knees." Joseph turned to Trent. "When Charlie was a teenager back in the States, we didn't realize we were swimming where there was a strong rip current, like quite a few beaches here in Liberia have. She got pulled farther and farther out and I couldn't get to her. Her mom and I kept yelling at her to relax and not fight the current, to just let it take her. Then swim horizontal to the shore until she came to a place without a rip so she could swim back in."

"Rip tides can be dangerous." Trent looked at Charlotte and saw her cheeks were flushed. Surely she wasn't embarrassed by something that happened when she was a kid? "Scary for anybody. But obviously you lived through it."

"Yes. I admit I thought for sure that was it,

though. That I was going to end up in the middle of the ocean and either drown or be devoured by a shark. So I just don't like going in the water."

"In the water? You don't even like getting in a small boat. Which has been a problem a few times," Joseph said. "You need to move past it and get your feet wet."

"Can we just drop this subject, please? I have a lot of work to do, anyway."

"Come to the beach, Charlotte," Trent said, wishing he could pull her into his arms and give her soothing kisses that would ease her embarrassment and the bad memory. "We'll work on getting you to move past your fear. You don't have to get in the water if you're not comfortable. But, you know, I did do a whole rotation in psychiatry at school. I'm sure I'm a highly qualified therapist." He gave her a teasing smile, hoping she'd relax and decide to come. Living with any kind of debilitating fear was no fun.

"Just go, Charlie," Joseph said. "It'll make me feel less guilty that I let you swim in that rip to begin with."

Charlotte gave an exaggerated sigh. "So this is about you now? Fine. I'll go. But I'm not promising to swim. I mean it."

"No promises needed," Trent said. "We can always just build a sandcastle so big that Princess Patience can walk inside."

"I like big sandcastles!" Patience beamed. "And In't care if we don't swim, Miss Charlie. Swimming isn't my favorite, anyway. We'll have fun on the beach."

"All right, then, that's settled," Joseph said. "John Adams and I will pack lunch while you get your things."

Trent grabbed swim trunks, a towel and his medical bag, which he'd learned always to have along on any excursion. Heading to the car, he had an instant vision of how Charlotte would look in a swimsuit: her sexy curves and smooth skin. Oh, yeah, he would more than enjoy a day at the beach with a beautiful woman; at the same time, he'd be glad to have chaperones to keep him from breaking his deal with her.

The thought of chaperones, though, didn't stop more compelling thoughts of swimming with Charlotte. How she'd feel in his arms when he held her close, trying to relieve her mind and soothe her fears, their wet bodies sliding together. How much he wished that, afterwards, they could lie on the hot sand and make love in the shade of a palm tree with the warm breeze tickling their skin.

Damn. His pulse kicked up and made him a little short of breath.

Chaperones were a very good thing.

CHAPTER ELEVEN

THE DRIVE THROUGH farms of papaya, mangoes and acres of rubber trees brought them to the soaring Grand Cape Mount, then eventually to the shoreline. Though John Adams had offered, Charlotte insisted on driving, of course. Trent had to wonder what made the woman feel a need to be in charge all the time. Didn't she ever want just to relax and go along for the ride?

Patience kept up a steady chatter until her father told her he'd give her a quarter if she could stay silent for five minutes. After she failed to manage that, Trent entertained her with a few simple card tricks he let her "win" that earned her the quarter after all.

They parked at the edge of the road and, as they unpacked their things from the car, Charlotte shook her head at Trent. "Is there a soul on the planet you can't charm to death?"

"To death? Doesn't exactly sound like you mean that in a nice way." Trent hooked a few beach chairs over his arm and they followed John Adams and Patience, who carried their lunches and a few plastic pails and shovels.

"Okay, charm, period. Everyone in the hospital thinks you're Mr. Wonderful."

"Does that include the director of the hospital?"

"Of course. I'm very grateful you filled in here—twice—until we can get another doctor."

Her voice had become polite, her smile a little stiff. Was she regretting that her rare time off had to be spent with him? Or could she be having the same problem he was having—wanting to take up where they'd left off at her house, knowing it was a hell of a bad idea?

As they approached the beach, Trent stopped to soak in the visual spectacle before him. A wide and inviting expanse of beige sand stretched as far as he could see, palm trees swaying in the ocean wind. A few houses sat off the shore, looking for all the world as though they were from the Civil War era of the deep south in the United States.

"How old do you think those houses are?" he asked Charlotte.

"Robertsport was one of the first colonies founded here by freed slaves. I think it goes back to 1829, so some of the houses here are over a hundred and fifty years old."

"That's incredible." He looked back down the beach and enjoyed the picturesque lines of fishermen with their seining nets stretched from the beach down into the water, about ten of them standing three feet apart, holding the nets in their hands. Several canoes sat on the shore, obviously made from a single hand-carved tree. One was plain, but the other was splashed with multiple colors of paint in an interesting hodgepodge design.

He was surprised to see a few surfers in the water farther down the beach, not too far from a cluster of black rocks in the distance. The waves were big and powerful, but were breaking fairly far out.

"I didn't know the people here surfed. I know Senegal is popular for surfing, but didn't know the sport had made its way here."

"I'm told an aid worker was here surfing maybe six or seven years ago. A local was fascinated and gave it a try. It's starting to take off, I guess, with locals competing and some tourists coming now."

"You know, we could always borrow a board from them. Want to give it a try?" he teased. The waves were pretty rough, so he knew there was no way she'd even consider it. The water closer to shore, though, was comparatively calm. Hopefully, he could get her into the lapping waves without it being too scary for her.

"Um, no. I think I'm going to be happy just beaching it, thanks anyway."

He'd have to see what he could do about changing her mind. They stopped in the middle of the wide beach and Charlotte laid some blankets on the soft sand. Patience tossed her toys and plopped down next to them. "Daddy, come help me build the castle!"

"How about we eat first, li'l girl?" John Adams said. "Miss Charlie and I brought some jollof rice, which I know you like. I don't know about everybody else, but I'm starving."

"You always starving, Daddy." The child grinned up at her father and Trent saw again what a strong bond there was between the two. The same kind of bond he'd seen grow so quickly between Chase and his son, even though he hadn't met them until the child was a toddler.

That surprising emotion tugged at Trent again, just as it had when Chase had told him about having a new little one on the way. A pinch of melancholy, knowing he'd likely never experience that kind of bond—though he knew only too well that not every family was as close as it seemed. That sometimes the chasm grew too large ever to be crossed.

After lunch and some sandcastle building, complete with a moat, Trent decided it was time to push Charlotte a little, to encourage her to face her fear. She was on her knees smoothing the last turret of the castle, and he pushed to his feet to stand behind her, smacking the sand from his hands. "Come on, Miss Edwards. Time for your psychotherapy session."

Immediately, her back stiffened. "I'm not done with the castle yet. Maybe later."

"Come on. It's hot as heck out here. Think how cool and refreshing the water will be."

"I'm going to watch Patience swim first." She turned to the little girl. "Remember you told me you wanted to learn to float in the lagoon? I want to see you."

And, if that wasn't an excuse, he'd never heard one. Obviously, it was going to be tough going getting her in the water.

John Adams grasped the child's hand and

pulled her to her feet. "Good idea. Come on, let's get in the lagoon and cool off."

The child's expression became even more worried than Charlotte's. "No, Daddy. I don't want to."

"Why not?"

She pointed at the lagoon water, separated from the ocean by about fifty feet of sand. "There's neegees in there. I don't want to get taken by the neegees."

"There's no neegees in there, I promise."

"For true, Daddy, there are. They talk about it at school." She stared up at her father with wide eyes. "The neegees are under the water and they grab people who swim. They suck people right out of the lagoon, and nobody knows where they go, and then they're never, ever seen again. Ever."

John Adams chuckled and pulled her close against his leg. "Sugar, I promise you. There's no such thing as neegees. Just like there's no witchcraft where someone can put a curse on you. All those are just stories. So let's get in the water and I'll help you learn to float."

Patience shook her head, pressing her face to her dad's leg. "No, Daddy. I'm afraid of the neegees."

Inspiration struck and Trent figured this was a good time to put those psych classes he'd teased Charlotte about to good use and solve two problems at once. "Patience, you know how Miss Charlie is afraid of the rip currents in the ocean? How she's afraid to go in the water too?"

The little girl peeked at him with one eye, the other still pressed against her father's leg. "Yes."

"How about if Miss Charlie decides she's going to get in the water even though she's afraid? Then, when you see how brave she is, and how she does just fine and has fun, you can get in the lagoon with your dad and have fun too. What do you say?"

Patience turned to look at Charlotte, whose expression morphed from dismay to serious irritation as she glared at Trent. He almost laughed, except he knew she was genuinely scared.

"I guess if Miss Charlie gets in the water and doesn't get bit by a shark then I can be brave too."

"Thanks for that encouragement, Patience. Now I really can't wait to swim," Charlotte said. She narrowed her eyes at Trent, green sparks flying. "And thank *you* for leaving me no choice here. I'll be back after I get my swimsuit on."

"I'll check out the rip situation before we go

in." Trent jogged into the water and leaped over the smaller waves before diving into a larger one. The water felt great and the inside of his chest felt about as buoyant as the outside. Charlotte was trusting him to help her feel safe in the water and he was going to do whatever he could to be sure she did.

Swimming parallel to the beach for a little in both directions, he didn't feel or see any major rips in the sand, though he'd still have to pay attention. Satisfied, he bodysurfed an awesome wave into shore, standing just in time to see Charlotte emerge from the path that led to the car.

Her beautiful body wore a pink bikini that wasn't super-skimpy but still showed plenty of her smooth skin and delectable curves. His pulse quickened and he reminded himself this little swim was supposed to make her feel safer and get past her fear. It was not an excuse to touch her all over.

Yeah, right. It was a damned great excuse, and not taking advantage of it was going to be nearly impossible.

"Ready?" He walked to her and stroked the pads of his fingers across the furrows in her brow, letting them trail softly down her cheek.

"Not really," she said under her breath. "But, since I'm now responsible for Patience not being afraid of the water for the rest of her life, I guess I have to be."

"I hope you're not mad at me. It's a good thing you're doing for her. And yourself." He grasped her hand and gave it a reassuring squeeze. "Don't worry. I'll be with you the whole time, and if you get really freaked out we'll head back in."

She nodded and gripped his hand tightly as they waded into the water, up to their knees, then her waist. In just another minute, the water was lapping at her breasts, which was so distracting he almost forgot to look for too-big waves that might be bearing down on them. He forced himself to look back at the ocean, making sure they weren't ending up in a dangerous spot, before returning his gaze to Charlotte's face. Her eyes were wide, the fear etched there clear, and he released her hand to put his arm around her waist, holding her close.

"I'm going to hold you now, so you feel more comfortable. Don't worry, I'm not getting creepy." He grinned and she gave him a weak smile in return. "In fact, why don't you get on my back and we'll just swim a little together that way until you feel more relaxed?"

"I admit I feel…uncomfortable. But I'm not a little kid, you know. Riding on your back seems ridiculous."

With that body of hers, there was no way she could be mistaken for a little kid. "Not if it makes you feel less nervous. Come on." He crouched down in the water up to his neck. "Get on, and wrap your arms around my throat. Just don't choke me if you get scared or we'll both drown," he teased.

To his surprise, she actually did, and he swam through the water with her clinging to him like a remora attached to a shark, enjoying the feel of the waves sluicing over his body. Enjoying the feel of her weight on him and of her skin sensuously sliding across his, just the way he'd fantasized.

"Okay?" he asked as a slightly bigger wave slapped into them, splashing water into their faces.

"Okay. I admit the water feels…nice."

"It does, doesn't it?" He grinned, relieved that this seemed to be working. "Ready to try a little on your own, with me holding your hand?"

"Um, I guess."

She slid from his back and, as she floated a foot or so away, her grim expression told him she wasn't anywhere near feeling relaxed. He took her hands and wrapped her arms behind his head, then placed his arms around her. Her face was so close, her mouth wet and parted as she breathed, her dripping hair glistening in streaks of bronze. He wanted, more than anything, to kiss her.

And, now that they were facing one another, pressed together, the sensuous feel of her soft breasts against his chest, of her legs sliding against his, was impossible to ignore. The sensation pummeled him far more than any wave could, and he battled back the raw need consuming him. He could only hope she couldn't feel his body's response to the overwhelming one-two punch that was delectable Charlotte Edwards.

"I...I'm not too freaked out, so that's good, isn't it?" Her voice was a bit breathless, but of course they were swimming a little, and treading water—though his own breath was short for a different reason.

"Yes. It's good." Holding her close was good. The feel of her body, soft and slick against his, was way better than good. He wanted to touch her soft satiny skin all over. Wanted to slide his hand inside her swimsuit top to cup her breast, to thumb the taut nipple he could feel poking against his chest. To slip his fingers inside her bikini bottom and caress her there, to see if she could possibly be as aroused as he was.

The world had shrunk to just the two of them floating in the water. Intensely focused on all those thoughts, Trent forgot to pay attention to the waves. A large whitecap broke just before it reached them, crashing into their bodies and en-gulfing them.

Charlotte shrieked and her wide, scared eyes met his just before the wave drove them toward shore. He held on to her, crushing her against him so she wouldn't get flung loose, and her arms squeezed around him in return, tightening be-hind his neck. "Hold on!" he said as the surf took them on a long, rapid, undulating ride to shore.

Pressed tightly together, they rode the wave, and as it flattened Trent rolled to be sure it was his back and not hers that scraped along the sandy bottom. They slid to a stop in about five inches of water, just a short distance from the dry shore. With Charlotte still clutched in his arms, Trent rolled again so she was beneath him, shielding her from the surf. The last thing he wanted was for a wave to hit her from behind and startle her before she could see it coming. He looked into her eyes as water dripped from his face and hair onto hers. "Are you all right?"

"Yes. I'm all right." She dragged in some air. "Though I think I know how a surfboard feels now. Or a piece of seaweed."

He chuckled, then glanced up to see that John Adams and Patience were in the lagoon, the child's little body lying flat with his hands supporting her as she practiced her floating.

With a grin, he looked back down at Charlotte. "Looks like it worked. You being brave helped Patience be brave. You even rode a wave into shore!"

"Only because I was attached to you." A little laugh left her lips and she smiled at him. One thick strand of hair lay across one eye and clung to her face and lips. "I'm glad Patience got in the lagoon. Funny; I kind of forgot to be scared, too. Because of you."

"You're just a lot braver than you give yourself credit for. Hell, you're the bravest woman I know, living in that house alone, doing what you're doing here. Being afraid of a rip tide after nearly drowning in one is normal. Just a tiny, human nick in that feisty spirit of yours." He lifted the strand away from her face as he looked at the little golden flecks in her eyes, her lashes stuck together with salt water. "I'm proud of you for facing that fear. For getting in the water even though you didn't want to." Tucking her hair behind her ear to join the rest that lay flat against her scalp, he suddenly saw something he'd never noticed before.

Her ear was oddly shaped—not just different, slightly abnormal. Nearly invisible scarring appeared on and around it. Probably no one without plastic surgery experience would be able to see it at all, but he could. He pressed his mouth to it, touching the contours of it with his lips and tongue.

"What happened to your ear?"

Her fingers dug into his shoulder blades. "My... ear? What do you mean?"

He let his mouth travel down her damp throat and back up to her jaw, because he just couldn't resist any longer; across her chin then up, slipping softly across her wet, salty lips before he lifted his gaze back to hers. "Your ear. Were you in an accident? Or was it something congenital?"

She was silent for a moment, just looking back at him, her eyes somber until she sighed. "Congenital. I was born with microtia."

"What grade of microtia? Was your ear just misshapen?"

"No, it was grade three. I only had this weird little skin flap that didn't look like an ear at all. We were told that's often accompanied by atresia, but I was blessed to have an ear canal, so I can hear pretty well out of it now."

"When did you have it reconstructed? Were you living in the States?"

She nodded. "I think doctors sometimes do the procedure younger now. But mine wanted to wait until I was nine, since that's when the ear grows to about ninety percent of its adult size." A small smile touched her mouth. "I still remember, when I was about five, why he told me I should be a little older before it was fixed—that it would look strange for a little girl to have a big, grown-up-sized ear, which at the time I thought was a pretty funny visual."

He gave her a soft kiss. "So you remember living with your ear looking abnormal?"

"Remember?" She gave a little laugh that had no humor in the sound at all. "Kids thought it was so hilarious to tease me about it. Called me 'earless Edwards.' One time a kid brought a CD to class for everyone to listen to, then said to me, 'Oh, right, you can't because you don't have an ear!' I wanted to crawl under my desk and hide."

He shook his head, hating that she'd had to go through that. "Kids can be nasty little things, that's for sure; convinced they're just being funny. Now I know where you got that chip on your shoulder from."

He was glad to see the shadows leave her eyes as she narrowed them at him, green sparks flying. "I do not have a chip on my shoulder. I just believe it's more efficient for me to drive and do whatever I need to do than take ten minutes talking about it just to dance around a man's ego."

"Good thing I'm so full of myself, which you've enjoyed telling me several times. Otherwise you would have crushed my feelings by now."

"As though I could possibly hurt your feelings."

"You might be surprised." And she probably would be, if she knew how rattled he'd felt for days. How much he wanted to leave while somehow, at the very same time, wanting to stay a little longer.

Her palms swept over his shoulder blades,

wrapped more fully around his back, and he took that as an invitation for another soft kiss. Her mouth tasted so good, salty-sweet and irresistible.

"Tell me more about your surgery." He lifted his finger to stroke the shell of it. "Did they harvest cartilage from your ribs to build the framework for the new ear?"

"Yes. I have a small scar near my sternum, but you can barely see it now. They finished it in three procedures."

"Well, it looks great. Whoever performed the surgery was very good at it. I bet you were happy."

"Happy?" Her smile grew wider. "I felt normal for the first time in my life. No longer the freak without an ear. It was…amazing."

Now it was all clear as glass. He pressed another kiss to her now smiling mouth. "I finally get why you built the plastic surgery wing, and why it's so important to you. You know firsthand how it feels to be scarred or look different from everyone else."

She nodded, her eyes now the passionately intense green he'd seen so often the past week; the passion that was such an integral part of who she was. "I know saving lives is important—more important than helping people view themselves differently, as you said. But I can tell you that feeling good about the way you look, not feeling like a freak, is so important to a person's psyche. And, even though I had to live for a while feeling like that, I know how blessed I was to have access to doctors who could make it better. You know as well as anyone that so many people around the world don't. And I want to give the people here, at least, that same opportunity to look and feel normal. Can you understand that?"

His answer was to stroke her hair from her forehead, cup her cheek in his palm and kiss her. From the minute he'd met her, she'd impressed him with her determination, and now he was even more impressed. She'd used a negative experience from her own life to try to make life better for others and worked damn hard to make it happen.

His tongue delved into her mouth, licking, tasting the ocean water and the flavor that was uniquely, delectably her. Tasting the passion that was so much a part of her. He was swept along by her to another place, deeper and farther and more powerfully than any wave could ever take him.

CHAPTER TWELVE

AS THE SURF lapped over their bodies, Charlie let herself drown in the kiss, in the taste of his cool, salty lips, his warm tongue deliciously exploring her mouth. Her hands stroked down his shoulder blades and back, reveling in the feel of the hard muscle beneath his smooth skin.

She tunneled her fingers into his thick, wet hair, wild and sexy and black as Liberian coal. His muscled thigh nudged between hers, sending waves of pleasure through every nerve. The taste of his mouth, the touch of his hands, the feel of his arousal against her took her breathlessly back to their incredible night of lovemaking.

"Charlotte," he whispered, his lips leaving hers to trail down her throat, to lick the water pooled there, then continuing their journey lower until his mouth covered her nipple, gently sucking on it through her wet nylon swimsuit.

She gasped. "Trent. That's so good. I—"

The sound of Patience laughing made her eyes

pop open as he lifted his head from her breast. His eyes— no longer the light, laughing blue she was used to seeing, but instead a glittering near-black—met hers. Everything about him seemed hard—his chest rising and falling against hers, his arms taut around her, his hips and what was between them.

"Charlotte," he said through clenched teeth. "More than anything, I want to make love to you right now. Right here. To wrap your legs around me and swim back into the waves; nobody would know I'm diving deep inside of you." His mouth covered hers in a steaming kiss. "But I guess that will have to wait until later."

If it hadn't already been difficult to breathe, his words nearly would have made her faint from the lack of oxygen in her brain. Even though she knew Patience and John Adams were fairly close by, she couldn't bring herself to move. The undulating water that wrapped around them was the most intimate cocoon she'd ever experienced in her life and she didn't want it to end. Couldn't find the will to detangle herself from his arms. "So I guess our deal is off."

"Our deal?"

"Not to start anything up again."

"Our deal has obviously been a challenge for me." His mouth lifted in a slow smile, his eyes gleaming. "Maybe we can come up with a slightly modified deal."

"Such as?"

His mouth traveled across her cheek, lowered to her ear. "We make love one more time. Cool down this heat between us and get it out of our systems. Then back to just colleagues for the last days I'm here so we won't have that second good-bye we both want to avoid."

The thought of one, just one more time with him, sent her heart into a crazy rhythm. "I agree to your terms. Just once."

"Just once. So—"

The sound of distant shouting interrupted him. They both turned their heads at the same time and saw a few of the surfers down the beach pulling what looked like an unconscious young man, or a body, from the water.

Trent sprinted down the beach with Charlotte on his heels.

Blood poured through the fingers of a young man sitting on the sand, holding his hand to his forehead. The group of surfers gathered around him looked concerned, and one shouted to another who was running to a mound of things they'd apparently brought with them. He returned with a shirt that he handed to the injured surfer, who pressed it to his head.

"Looks like you need a hand here," Trent said as he approached the injured boy. "I'm a doctor. Will you let me take a look?"

"You a doctor?" The young man looked utterly surprised, and no wonder. There weren't too many doctors around there, period, and it was just damned good luck he happened to be on the beach when the kid was hurt.

"Yes. I work at the Edwards Mission Hospital. This lady is the director." He smiled at Charlotte, now standing next to him, before crouching down. "What's your name? Will you show me what we're dealing with here?"

"Murvee Browne," he replied, lowering his hand with the now-bloody shirt balled up in it. "I was surfing and, when the board flipped, I think the fin got me."

"Looks like it." Trent leaned closer to study the wound. It was one damned deep gash, probably five centimeters, stretching from the hairline diagonally across his forehead to his eyebrow. The injury appeared to slice all the way to the skull, but it was a little hard to tell while it was still bleeding so much. He'd let the kid know it was serious, but reassure him so he wouldn't freak out at what he was going to have to do to repair it. "You've got a pretty good one there. But at least it's just your forehead. I took care of one nasty surf accident victim where the guy's eyelid was slit open too."

Murvee grimaced while his friends gathered even closer to stare at the gash.

"You did it good, oh!" one friend said. "You so lucky the doctor is here today."

Murvee looked worried as he stared at Trent. "What you charge for fixing me up, doc? I don't make much. My mother makes money at the market, but she needs what I have to help take care of my brothers and sisters."

"Why don't you press that cloth against your forehead real firmly again and keep it there to stop the bleeding, okay, Murvee?" Chase said. "You don't have to worry about paying me. Miss Charlotte here pays me a lot, and she gets mad if I don't do any work to earn it."

He shot a teasing glance at her and she rolled her eyes in return, but there was a smile in them too. "We're going to have to have a little talk about your spreading rumors of what a tyrant I am," she said.

He chuckled and turned his attention back to Murvee. "Are you feeling okay? Not real dizzy or anything?"

"No. I feel all right."

"I'd like to take you back to the hospital to get you stitched up."

"No hospital." Murvee frowned, looking mulish. "I have to be home soon and I have to go to work. I can just have my mom fix it."

"Murvee…"

"How about stitching him in the jeep?" Charlotte suggested, giving him a look that said he was going to have to be flexible here. "I know you brought your bag with you. I'll help any way I can."

Trent sighed. He knew taking Murvee to the hospital and getting his wound taken care of there would take hours, and likely be tough on his family—if he could get the kid to go at all. "Fine. Since you seem okay other than the gash, I won't insist. Let's go to the car."

Murvee's friends helped him stand and the three of them headed down the beach. Trent kept an eye on the young man as they trudged to the car, and he thankfully did seem to be feeling all right, not shocked or woozy. Charlotte opened the back of her banged-up SUV and they worked together to get the kid situated inside and lying on a blanket with his feet propped up on the side beneath the window before Trent grabbed his medical bag.

"What do you need me to do first?" Charlotte asked.

"Did you bring any fresh water I can wash it out with? And are all the towels sandy, or do we have a clean one?" he asked.

"I brought extra towels. And I have water."

"Good." He turned to Murvee. "Let me see if the bleeding has stopped." The young man lifted away the shirt; the bleeding had, thankfully, lessened. Trent got everything set up as best he could in the cramped space, putting his flashlight, gauze, Betadine, local anesthetic and suture kit next to the young man. Squeezing out some of the sanitizer he always kept in his bag, he thoroughly rubbed it over his hands and between his fingers then snapped on gloves.

"Here's the water and towels." Charlotte came

to stand next to him, knees resting against the bumper of the car. "What else can I do?"

He looked at her, standing there completely calm, and marveled again that she took on any task thrown at her calmly and efficiently. Including dealing with a bleeding gash that would look so awful to most non-medical professionals, it might make them feel a little faint, or at least turn away so they wouldn't have to look at it.

"You want to wash out the wound to make sure it's good and clean before I suture it? Put the folded towel under his head. After I inject the lidocaine, I want you to pour a steady stream of the water through the wound." He drew the anesthetic into the syringe. "You still doing all right, Murvee? I'm going to give you some numbing medicine. I have to use a needle, and it'll burn a little, but you won't feel the stitches."

Murvee held his breath and winced a few times as he injected it. "Sorry. I know this hurts, but pretty soon it will feel numb."

"I don't care, doc. I'm very grateful to you for helping me."

"I'm glad we were here today." He'd felt that way on many occasions in his life, since this kind of thing seemed to happen fairly often when he was working in the field, or even like today when he was touring and relaxing. Which was why he'd become convinced that whatever higher power was out there truly had a hand in the workings of the universe.

"Am I doing this right?" Charlotte asked as she continued washing out the wound.

"Perfect." He studied it, satisfied that it looked pretty clean now. "I think we're good to go. Thanks." He squeezed a stream of antiseptic on gauze then brushed it along the wound's edges.

Trent saw Charlotte reach for the young man's hand and give it a squeeze. "Tell me about surfing, Murvee. How long have you been doing it?"

"Me and my friends surf for a year now. A guy from the UK was surfing here a while ago and he was really good. He showed some people how to surf, and now many of us do. I want to get good enough to compete in the Liberian Surfing Championships, which has been around about five years now, I think."

Trent glanced at Charlotte again as he got the suture materials together, smiling at the warm and interested expression on her face. He loved the many facets to her personality: the feisty fireball, the take-charge director, the soft and sexy woman whose love-making he knew would stay in his memory a long, long time and the person he was seeing now. She was nurturing and caring for this young man, distracting him with casual chit-chat so Murvee wouldn't think too hard about the time-consuming procedure Trent was about to do on him.

He nodded at his small but powerful flashlight and looked at Charlotte. "Will you shine that on the wound so I can see better?" They were parked within the trees and, while it was far from optimal conditions for suturing, the flashlight illuminated well enough.

She pointed the light at the wound. "Does that help?"

"Yes, great," he said as he began suturing. It was deep and would require a three-layer closure. The boy was lucky a medic was here today. While the injury would likely have healed eventually on its own, his scars would have been bold and obvious, not to mention there was a good chance the wound would have become infected, maybe seriously.

"You should see the way your head looks, Murvee. You want to check it out in a mirror, so you can watch what Dr. Trent has to do to repair that nasty gash?"

"I don't know about that, Charlotte." Trent frowned at her in surprise. Trust a non-medical assistant to come up with a wacky idea like that, though it was probably because, if she'd had a wound that required suturing, Ms. Toughness would have wanted to watch.

"I would like to see," Murvee said. "I want to tell my friends what you had to do, what it looked like."

"So long as you don't faint on me." He smiled at the young man, who gave him a nice smile in return that seemed pretty normal and not particularly anxious.

Charlotte held up a small mirror in a powder compact and Murvee took it from her, moving his head around so he could see himself.

"Please hold still, Murvee." When this was over, he was going to give Charlotte a few pointers on doctor-assisting. She'd done a great job helping the boy relax, but this wasn't helping *him*, though he had to appreciate the ingenuity in her distraction techniques. If the boy didn't get queasy, that was.

"What exactly you doing?" Murvee asked as

he looked at Trent suturing his wound in the mirror, seeming fascinated, thankfully, instead of disturbed.

Since the kid asked, he figured he might as well give him the full details. "Your wound was so deep I could see some of your skull bone."

Murvee's eyes widened. "No kidding?"

"No kidding. I repaired the galea first—that's the layer that covers the bone. Now I'm sewing up the layer under the skin—we call it the subcutaneous tissue, or 'sub-Q.' You've got some very healthy sub-Q."

"Yeah, man. Fine sub-Q." He grinned, obviously proud, and Trent and Charlotte both laughed. "That's crazy-looking," Murvee said, staring into the mirror.

"The whole human body is kind of crazy-looking. One of the cool things about being a doctor is learning about how crazy it really is. And amazing."

Murvee looked at him then and Trent was glad the boy finally lowered the mirror. "Is my head going to look like this always, doc?"

"Not always." He gave Charlotte a look that she interpreted correctly, thank goodness, since she took the mirror from Murvee and tucked it into her purse. "After I finish, you'll look a little like Frankenstein, and your friends will be jealous of how cool and tough you look." He smiled, knowing from experience that boys and young men related to that and were usually amused. "But by sewing it in three steps using very tiny stitches it will heal well and, over time, the scar will become a thin line. You'll be as handsome as ever and all the girls will think you're great."

Murvee grinned at Trent's commentary, as he'd expected. "Girls think I'm great already."

The sound of Charlotte's little laugh brought their attention back to her. "I bet they do," she said. "And now you can talk to them about how you were hit by your board while you were surfing, which not many guys around here do, and ended up getting stitched up on the beach by a world-class surgeon."

"World-class?" Trent smiled, wondering if she'd really meant that, or if she was just talking to keep Murvee relaxed as he worked. Wondering why it felt nice for her to say it, when he'd always been sure he didn't need anyone's admiration or accolades.

"Are you kidding me?" Her green eyes met his and held, a brief moment of connection that warmed him in a totally different way than she'd warmed him in the water. "You're amazing. With technique like yours, you could be working as a plastic surgeon in Beverly Hills."

"Which would be your idea of having really made it, right?" Concentrating on suturing Murvee, disappointment jabbed at him that she apparently felt that way. He'd been there and done the Beverly Hills-type vanity plastic surgery and rejected it for a reason. A reason nobody understood or cared about.

"Is that a real question?" Charlotte asked, her expression one of annoyed disbelief. "If my idea of 'making it' was a Beverly Hills lifestyle, I'd have set my sights on a big hospital in the States after I got my degrees or gone to work on Wall Street. Not come to Liberia."

He looked back up at her. He should have realized her comment had just been intended as a light-hearted compliment. She was as far from a New York City or Beverly Hills socialite as a woman could be. "I know you haven't exactly chosen glamour over substance here. Except those pretty, polished toenails of yours could be considered pretty glamorous."

"Does that mean you like them? I changed the

color last night." She smiled as their eyes met again and lingered.

"Yeah. I like them." He looked back down and continued the detailed suturing of Murvee's wound, trying to focus on only his work and not her lethal combo of femininity and toughness.

"Do you mind if I take a photograph of your injury, Murvee?" Charlotte asked.

When he agreed, she snapped a number of pictures and Trent wondered what she planned to use them for. Probably to put in a portfolio of the plastic surgery wing. Except it wasn't open yet.

Trent gave the young man some antibiotic tablets and instructions on how to take care of the wound.

"I know the hospital's a long way off. Any way you can get there in a week? I probably won't be there anymore, but there are several great techs who can remove your stitches. I'd also like you to have a tetanus shot."

"My family has a scooter, so I can come. Thank you again for everything." He pumped Trent's hand then reached for Charlotte's too, a smile so wide on his face you'd never have known the injury he'd just suffered if you hadn't seen the bandage on his head.

"You're very welcome. Like I said, I'm glad we were here today."

The young man headed back down the beach. Charlotte looked at Trent and the expression in her eyes made his breath hitch. He reached for her hand. "Ready, Miss Edwards?"

"Yes. I'm ready to head back."

He was pretty sure she knew that heading back to the compound wasn't what he'd been asking.

CHAPTER THIRTEEN

DARKNESS HAD NEARLY enfolded the hospital compound as Charlie pulled the car up to her house. When she'd dropped Trent off at his quarters, the look he'd given her before he'd walked away was sizzling enough practically to set her hair on fire.

Both excited and nervous, her insides felt all twisted around, thinking about her subterfuge with his release papers, the new doctor and all the things she was trying to manipulate. But all that worry wasn't quite enough to douse cold water on her plans. To keep her from wanting to relive, one more time, the passionate thrill of the night they'd spent locked in one another's arms the previous week.

Still sitting in her car with the engine off, she stared at a small impediment to that plan, all too clearly apparent in the lights that were currently burning in her house. Her dad was staying with her and wasn't leaving for another day or two.

Which meant that her house as a rendezvous for Trent and her to make love all night was out. Her mind spun with ideas of where else they might meet, though it couldn't be from now into the morning. The various possibilities, and the memories of their past love-making, had her ready to leap out of the car to run and pound on the man's door, despite the fact that she'd dropped him off only minutes ago.

Had she suddenly become a sex maniac? The thought made her laugh at herself, at the same time her anticipation ratcheted higher. For whatever reason, the secretiveness added a certain allure; why that was, she didn't know. But she wasn't going to fight the excitement she felt, because she knew she'd only get to enjoy it one more time.

The real question was, should she go inside and have dinner with her dad, take a shower to wash off the beach then find an excuse to leave again? Or just not come back until later? Her dad had encouraged her to take time off today, after all. Maybe he'd just assume they'd made a long day of it in Robertsport.

Except he'd know that wasn't true, because Patience had been with them and would be ready for bed very soon.

She shook her head at her ambivalence, reminding herself that she was twenty-seven years old and a grown woman. Her father wasn't naive or judgmental. Shoving open the car door, she decided she'd just go in and say hello, then tell him she had dinner plans with Trent; never mind that there couldn't be a candlelit dinner in a restaurant, just leftovers in the hospital kitchen.

The sound of her father's favorite jazz music met her as she opened the front door. He sat in one of the upholstered chairs she'd bought when she'd moved here, since little of the original furniture had survived the pillaging during the wars. The hospital files were open on his lap and he looked up with a smile as she entered the room.

"Did my girl get in the water today?"

"I did. I even rode a wave all the way in to shore. How about that?"

He clapped his hands. "Bravo! I'm proud of you. And not just for swimming today. For all you've done here." He gestured to the files. "I'm so impressed with what you've accomplished with the funding you have. You're making huge headway, especially considering the shambles you were left to work with."

"Thanks, Dad. That means a lot to me." When her parents had trusted her to bring the hospital and school back to life, it had been scary and admittedly daunting. But, with John Adams's help, they'd done a lot. And she had to admit she felt pretty proud of what they'd accomplished too.

"I know the plastic surgery wing is important to you, and of course I understand why." His expression was filled with both sympathy and pain. "You had to deal with a lot as a little girl."

"Things happen for a reason, Dad. You know that as well as anyone. I hope that experiencing what it feels like to look abnormal will end up helping people who have to deal with things a whole lot worse than my childhood embarrassment."

"I do know. And I'm excited about your project. But I have to ask some hard questions now, not as a father, but as a businessman. And this has to be treated like a business."

Uh-oh. She gulped, afraid she knew what was coming next. "What are your hard questions?"

"What happens if, by some stroke of bad luck,

the Gilchrist Foundation money doesn't come through? Do you have a backup plan?"

She closed her eyes for a moment, wondering how she should answer. Should she tell him she'd known all along that it was a risk? That maybe it was a risk she shouldn't have taken? She forced herself to open her eyes and tell him the truth. "Honestly? No. I don't. If the foundation money doesn't come through, we're in serious trouble. I'm trying to solicit other sources of income, but none of it is for sure until we have it in our hands."

He nodded. "All right. So when will you know about the foundation money?"

"Soon. They're sending their rep here in the next few days to see if we meet their requirements."

"And I see that you've met all those requirements except for one: a plastic surgeon on site."

"I *do* have a plastic surgeon on site—Trent. I just need for him to stay until their representative gives us the green light. Then we'll have the Gilchrist check and it'll all be good."

He looked at her steadily. "Except that something tells me Trent doesn't know about all this."

For once, she wished her dad wasn't so darned

intuitive. "No. He doesn't. I don't see any reason for him to know."

"Why not? Seems to me he's an important part of the equation."

"Only for a short time. He performed a brilliant plastic surgery on a boy here in the hospital and another today on the beach that I can show pictures of." She sucked in a fortifying breath so she could continue. "He doesn't want to be involved, Dad. For some reason, he doesn't want to perform plastic surgeries. But I'm still hoping he'll agree to help a few patients with serious problems before he leaves."

"He seems like a good man. You should tell him the truth."

The truth? Her dad didn't know about the lies she'd told and her stomach twisted around when she thought about what his reaction would be if he did. If he'd still be as proud of her as he said he was. "I'm handling it, Dad. It will turn out okay; we'll get the funding." And she prayed that would really happen and every problem would be solved.

"I hope you're right. Now, there's something else we need to talk about, Charlie." Her father threaded his fingers together in his lap and looked at her. "Your goals are worthy goals. Your hard work is to be commended. But have you ever asked yourself if there's more you need to consider?"

"Such as?"

"Your own life." He stood and placed his hands on her shoulders. "Have you thought about exploring a relationship with a man who lives here? Or one of the single doctors coming through? Trent has impressed me, and I've met Perry Cantwell—who's coming soon, I think you said. He's nice enough, and good-looking to boot. I know it's damned difficult to meet someone when you live and work where there aren't too many folks around. I don't want to see you give everything of yourself for this place until there's nothing left of you to share with anyone else. I've seen it happen and I don't want it to happen to you."

"It won't. I promise. I just need to get that wing open and the place running smoothly then I'll think of other things besides work. I will."

And that was the truth. Even in the midst of this serious conversation with her dad, and all the stress over the hospital's finances, thoughts of Trent were foremost in her mind, thoughts of meeting with him and finishing what they'd started this afternoon. All those thoughts sent her breathing haywire and her pulse skipping and she just wanted to end this conversation and be with him.

"In fact, Dad, Trent and I are going to have a late dinner over in the hospital. Are you okay here eating leftovers on your own?"

His serious and worried expression gave way to a big smile. "Of course. Leftovers are my favorite."

"Good." She kissed his cheek then gave him a fierce hug. She wouldn't tell her dad that the thought of giving up her freedom forever, her ability to live as she wanted and do as she wanted and run the hospital as she wanted, sent a cold chill down her spine. Or that one more wonderful night with Trent just might be enough to satisfy her relationship needs for a long, long time. "Thanks for the advice, Dad."

"Okay." He hugged her back just as fiercely. "Go on, now."

The night air embraced Charlie with a close, sultry warmth as she walked toward the hospital quarters. A huge gibbous moon hung in the sky, casting a glow of white light across the earth. Her feet moved in slow, measured steps, her dad's words echoing in her head.

Could there possibly ever be anything between her and Trent other than physical pleasure and friendship, a friendship based on both of their experiences working in developing nations and an appreciation of the tremendous need there?

No. She shook her head in fervent denial. What the two of them had experienced during their one night together was what anyone would feel after being focused on only work for months and months. What Trent no doubt felt for all the various women in his life, which if rumor was to be believed were many. He was famous in the GPC community for enjoying short and no doubt very sweet interludes until he moved on to his next job.

She could deal with that. After all, hadn't she known it from the start? Enjoying one more night of fantastic sex with a special man would be wonderful, just as it had been last week, without thoughts of tomorrows and futures and what any of it might mean.

The employee quarters loomed gray in the darkness, its roof lit by moonlight, and her steps faltered, along with her confidence. He'd said he wanted to be with her just one more time, hadn't he? She could only hope, now that they were on dry land and no longer only half-dressed, a knock on his door wouldn't bring the cool Trent who sometimes appeared. The one who had shown very clearly how little he wanted to be stuck with her in this little, forgotten place in Liberia.

A shadowy figure suddenly became visible in front of her and she nearly let out a small shriek at the apparition.

"Charlotte? Is that you?"

"Yes." She exhaled at the sound of Trent's low voice, blaming the surprise of his sudden appearance for her weak and breathy reply. "I was… coming to see if you wanted to find some dinner in the kitchen."

"Now there's a surprise—you being hungry again. Let's see what we can do about that." Through the darkness, she saw the gleam of his eyes for what seemed like barely a second before he moved fast and was there, right in front of her, his arms wrapping around her, pulling her close. Before she could barely blink, he was kissing her.

And kissing her. His mouth possessed hers in a thorough exploration that stole her breath. Not rushed, but intense and deep, giving and taking, completely different from his teasing, playful kisses of before. Every hard inch of him seemed to be touching her at once, his chest pressing against her breasts, his thighs to her hips, his taut arms against her back.

A small moan sounded in her throat as his mouth devoured hers. She wanted this: wanted this sensory explosion; wanted his kisses and touch and the heat that crawled and burned across her skin.

His mouth left hers, softly touching her eyelids, her nose, her lips, stealing her breath. "You taste so good to me, Charlotte. Way better than any food, though I have a feeling that the more I taste you, the hungrier I'm going to get."

"Me too. Food is overrated." He tasted so delicious, so wonderful, so right. His lips and tongue returned to her mouth with an expertise that dazzled, so mind-blowing that her skin tingled, her knees got wobbly and, if he hadn't been holding her so tightly, they might have simply crumpled beneath her.

She flattened her palms against the firm contours of his chest, up to his thick, dark hair that was getting a little long, and the feel of its softness within her fingers was as sensual as the feel of his body pressed to hers.

The little moan she heard this time came from him, and he pulled his mouth from hers, his heartbeat heavy against her breasts. "Charlotte." His hands roamed across her back and down to her bottom, pulling her so close that his erection pressing against her stomach nearly hurt. "Do you have any idea how hard it's been for me to keep my distance this week? Not to come into your office and lock the door and make love to you right on top of your desk?"

She might have had some idea, since the thought of knocking on the door of his quarters had crossed her mind more than once when she'd been sitting alone in her house, lying alone in her bed. "On top of my desk? It's a little small, don't you think?"

"Probably." She could see the adorable, perpetual gleam of humor behind the sexual glint in his eyes. "And the examination table is too narrow. My bed is small, too, and pretty squeaky at that. Which leaves us with finding a soft place on the ground beneath the stars tonight."

"I hope you're not thinking of making love in the mud. That sounds a little….messy."

He kissed her again, his hands moving to her waist, up her ribs, stopping for a breathless moment just beneath her breasts before moving up to cup them both. They tightened and swelled within his palms, and she wanted to be done with the talking and drag him to the ground.

"I have the place already picked out, with a thick blanket already unfolded on the ground. After I make love to you, we'll take a shower together." His lips moved to her ear, his voice a hot whisper that sent shivers skating across her flesh. "I want to taste the sea on you, lick the salt from your skin. Wash every inch of you and start all over again."

Her heart pounded so hard in her ears, she thought he just might be able to feel the vibration on his tongue as he traced it over the shell of her ear. Her breath was coming in short gasps, and she was burning up inside, wanting him more than she'd ever wanted anything in her life.

"What about dinner?" Goodness, she could barely talk. "You must be hungry."

"For you. Most definitely hungry for you." The expression in his eyes told her he wanted her every bit as much as she wanted him, and she loved that she could make him feel that way. "But

I know about that stomach of yours. I have a picnic dinner all ready in my room. For later."

She managed a small laugh. "How did you find time to do all that?"

"I had powerful motivation to move fast." His lips touched one corner of her mouth, then the other, and she found herself chasing after them for a real kiss.

"So where is this blanket? If we don't go there soon, my knees will be too weak to walk."

"Not a problem." He released her and quickly swung her into his arms. A squeak of surprise left her lips and he pressed his mouth to hers as he strode through the darkness. "Quiet." His eyes, now dark, glittered with both passion and amusement. "You want somebody in the hospital quarters to investigate a possible murder? Or your dad?"

"No. Though you are about killing me here." She wrapped her arms around his neck and pressed her mouth to his throat. "How far do we have to go?"

"Are you talking about where the blanket is? It's close." His eyes, glinting, met hers. "But if you're talking about something else, the answer is, as far as we possibly can."

His words made her laugh at the same time as a wave of hot need enveloped her. A need to experience another unforgettable night as exhilarating as the one they'd shared before.

He carried her deeper into the palm forest then stopped. She glimpsed the blanket lying open on the ground before he released her, letting her body slowly slide down his until she stood teetering slightly on her own feet, her dress bunched up to her hips where he still held on to her.

The dress bunched higher, slipping up her torso as he tunneled his hands beneath it until it was up and off of her. Until she stood in only her white bra and panties, and the misty touch of the moonlight made them seem to glow in the darkness. He looked at her, and even through the low light she could see the heat in his gaze, the tautness of his jaw, and her body throbbed for him.

"Do you have any idea how beautiful you are?" His voice was low, rough, and he lifted one hand to trace his finger along the lacy edge of her bra. "The very first moment I saw you in your office, I wanted to know what you looked like naked. And when you gave me that gift, it was more amazing than I could ever have dreamed."

He lowered his mouth to hers, one hand closing

over her breast. The other cupped her waist then deliciously stroked along her ribs and down over her bottom covered in only her thin panties. She gasped at the pleasure of it. How had she managed to keep him at arm's length for the past few days? And, as his touch caressed her, thrilled her, she wondered why she had.

She broke the kiss to fumble with the buttons on his shirt, wanting to feel his skin too. Wanting to run her fingers across the hardness of his muscles, the surprising silkiness of his skin, the soft, dark hair covering it. "You know what I thought was the sexiest thing about you when we first met?" she asked.

"My amazing intelligence?" The teasing look was back in his eyes, along with a sexual gleam that intensified the ache between her legs.

"Your hands. Those long surgeon's fingers of yours. I just had a feeling they were very, very talented. Little did I know exactly how talented, with your plastics skills and magic skills and piano skills."

"And other skills." His lips curved and with a quick, deft movement, he flicked open her bra and slid it from her arms. "I'm looking forward to showing you some you haven't seen yet."

She wished her fingers were as magical as his as she struggled to get the last of the annoying buttons undone. Finally, finally, she was able to shove his shirt from his shoulders to see his muscled chest. She flattened her hands against it, loving the feel of it, thrilling in the quick, hard beat of his heart against her palms. "Oh, yeah? Like what?"

"Showing is always better than telling." He shucked his pants and underwear until he stood fully naked, the moonlight illuminating the broadness of his shoulders, his lean hips, his strong thighs and the powerful arousal between them.

"Hmm. Is this what you wanted to show me?" Desire for him nearly buckled her knees and she decided to take matters into her own hands, so to speak. She reached for him as she kissed him, stroking him, teasing him, and she felt him respond with a deep shudder. A low groan sounded in his throat. His hands tightened on her back and his fingers dug into her bottom until it nearly hurt.

"Not exactly. Oh, Charlotte." There was a ragged hitch to the way he said her name, and in the next breath he practically pushed her down onto the blanket, kissing her, covering her body with his heavy warmth that felt impossibly familiar, considering how short their time had been together the week before.

His fingers teased her nipples, glided slowly down, over her ribs, her belly, then lower. They slipped slowly, gently in and around the moist and slick juncture between her thighs; the sensation was most definitely magical. She couldn't control the movement of her hips as they reached for his talented fingers, sought more of the erotic sensation he gave her.

She needed more. Needed all of him. "Now, please, Trent. I want you now."

"If I could say no, not yet, I would. But, damn it, I can't wait any longer to be inside of you." Propped onto his elbows, he stared down at her. The intensity in his blue eyes held hers, mesmerized, as she opened for him, welcomed him. And, when he joined with her, it felt so wonderful, so familiar and yet so new all at the same time.

Rhythmically, they moved together, faster and deeper, until the earth seemed a part of them and the night stars seemed to burst into an explosion of light. And as she gave herself over to the pleasure of being in his arms, to the ecstasy of being at one with him, she cried out. He covered her mouth with his, swallowing the sounds of both of them falling.

For a long while, they lay there together as they caught their breath and their heart rates slowed. His face was buried in her neck. His weight felt wonderful pressing her into the soft earth, and she made a little sound of protest as he eventually rolled off her, keeping her hand entwined with his.

Still floating in other-worldly sensation, the sound of his laughter surprised her. She turned her head to look at him. "What's so funny?"

"Looks like we managed to lose the blanket." Despite the darkness, his eyes met hers, his teeth gleaming white as he grinned. "I guess we made love in the mud after all."

She looked down and realized that they were, indeed, squished down into the mud; how they hadn't noticed that, she couldn't imagine. Actually, she could. Her mind slipped back to how wonderful it had been to be with him again, and just thinking about it made her feel like rolling her muddy body on top of him.

So she did, and he laughed again as she smeared a handful of mud on his chest and stomach then wriggled and squished against him. "I think I like it. Don't people pay good money for mud baths?"

"They do. I'm pretty sure pigs like mud too."

"Are you calling me a pig?"

He gave her a lazy, relaxed smile as he stroked more cool mud over and across her bottom, which felt so absurdly, deliciously sensual she couldn't help wriggling against him a little more. "I've been around enough women in my life to never, ever say anything that stupid."

The thought of all the women he'd had in his life shouldn't have had the power to bring the pleasure of the moment down, but somehow it did. Which was silly, since she knew the score, didn't she?

Something of her thoughts must have shown in her expression, because he wiped his muddy hand on the blanket then stroked her hair back from her face, all traces of amusement gone. "I have been to a lot of places and known a lot of people." He tucked her hair behind the ear her plastic surgeon had created for her then traced it softly, tenderly, with his finger. "But you're special. I've never met anyone who is such an incredible combination of sexiness, compassion and take-no-prisoners toughness. You amaze me. Truly."

"Thank you." Her heart swelled at his sweet words and she used her one not-muddy hand to cup his cheek as she leaned down to give him a soft kiss. "You amaze me too. Truly."

"And I can tell you that, if I was going to fund a school or a hospital anywhere, I'd trust you to run it." Through the moonlit darkness, his eyes stared into hers with a deep sincerity. "I'd trust you with anything."

Damn. His words painfully clutched at her heart and twisted her stomach, making her feel slightly sick. He'd trust her with anything?

She could only hope and pray he never found out exactly how misplaced that trust really was.

CHAPTER FOURTEEN

THE DELICIOUS PICNIC Trent had put together for them, complete with a bottle of wine he said he'd tucked in his bag for the right moment, was the most intimate and lovely meal Charlie had experienced in her life. It didn't matter that they'd both been curled up on his skinny bed, towels wrapped around and beneath their muddy bodies, and that the wine "glasses" had been plastic cups.

After they'd eaten, the pleasure of the shower they'd shared—laughing as they'd washed the mud off their bodies, then no longer laughing as they enjoyed making love again within the erratic spray of water—wasn't quite enough to make Charlie completely forget his words. To forget his misplaced trust in her. To remember her conviction that the end was worth the means.

She'd hardly slept after she'd crept into her house and fallen into her bed, tired, wired and worried. And still she ended up back at her desk as the sun rose. She stayed closeted in her office much of the day, contacting every potential donor, digging everywhere she could to possibly find some cash commitments in case the Gilchrist donation fell through.

Thankfully, the hospital and clinic had been busy too so she and Trent hadn't seen one another except when he'd passed by her accidentally left-open door, giving her a sexy, knowing smile and a wink.

Deep in thought, a knock on the now closed door startled her. "Come in." She readied herself to see a tall, hunky doctor with amused blue eyes, but relaxed when her dad appeared.

"Hi, honey. Have a second?"

"Of course."

He settled himself in the only other chair in her tiny office. "I've decided to head on home tonight, instead of waiting until tomorrow. Your mom called to say a church group has sent a few members to study our school, and I'd like to be there to talk with them when they get there."

"I understand, Dad. I'm planning to come see you and Mom soon for a few days anyway, as soon as…things are settled here." No point in starting up another conversation about the hospital funding and potential problems there. She stood and rounded the desk, leaning down to kiss his cheek. "But you should wait until tomorrow morning. Why in the world would you drive at night on these roads if you don't have to?"

"I'm stopping on the way. Do you remember Emmanuel and Marie? I'm going to visit them and check out their school, which is just across the border in the Ivory Coast. I'm staying there a day, then heading home." He threaded his fingers together like he always did when he had something serious to say, and she braced herself. "Will you remember what I said about not giving everything to this place? About being open to the possibilities that may come along in your personal life? Think about giving Perry Cantwell a fair shot."

"Does Charlotte have a personal life with Perry Cantwell?"

She swung around and stared at Trent leaning casually against the doorjamb, a smile on his face. But his eyes were anything but amused. They looked slightly hard and deadly serious.

A nervous laugh bubbled from her throat. The man was leaving in a matter of days. Surely he wasn't jealous of some possible future relationship with his replacement? "I've never even met

Perry Cantwell. But seems to me you've been anxious for him to get here so you could leave. Maybe I'm anxious for him to get here, too."

It wasn't nice to goad him like that after what they'd shared together last night and she knew it. But her emotions were all over the place when it came to Trent: needing him to stay until the Gilchrist rep came; wanting him to stay because she'd grown closer to him than was wise, closer than she should have allowed. This looming goodbye was going to be so much harder than the first one, as she'd worried all along it would be. And added to that was the fear that he'd somehow find out about her machinations, destroying the trust, the faith, he said he had in her.

Which shouldn't really have mattered, since he'd be out of her life all too soon. But somehow it mattered anyway. A lot.

His posture against the doorjamb relaxed a little, as did the cool seriousness in his eyes. His lips curved as he shook his head, but that usual twinkle in his eyes was still missing. "Perry's a good surgeon, but I hear he cheats at golf. Talks down to nurses. Sometimes dates men. Not a good fit for you, Charlotte."

"I'm pretty sure you're making all that up."

She stepped back to her desk and rested her rear end against it. "Dad's right that I need to keep all possibilities open—except maybe not men who date men."

Her dad chuckled, which reminded her he was there. "I've got to get going before it gets any later. Will you stay with Charlie tonight, Trent? I know we haven't had any sign of burglars since before I got here, but I'd feel better if we gave it a few more nights."

"Dad, I don't—"

"Of course I will. You didn't have to ask; I would've been there, anyway."

The smoldering look he gave her both aroused and embarrassed her, and she hoped her father didn't see it, along with the blush she could feel filling her cheeks. Though she had a feeling her dad wouldn't exactly be surprised to know that she and Trent were a little more than just acquaintances and colleagues.

Her father stood. The small smile on his face told her he'd seen Trent's look and was more than aware of the sizzle between them. She blushed all over again. "I need to grab my files before I go." He looked at the various piles on her desk and frowned, lifting up one or two. "I thought they were right here. Did you move them?"

"I put them—" Oh no; he had his hands on the pile she'd shoved Trent's release papers into, practically right in front of the man! Why, oh why hadn't she buried them deep in a drawer? She hastily reached to grab them. "Don't mess with that pile, Dad. Yours are—"

And because she was so nervous and moving too fast, and karma was probably getting back at her, the middle of the pile slid out and thunked on the floor, with some of the papers fluttering around Trent's feet.

He reached down to gather the mess and she feared she just might hyperventilate. Snatching them up and acting even stranger than she was already would just raise suspicion, so she forced herself to quickly but calming retrieve and stack the files. Until her heart ground to a stop when she saw Trent had a paper in his hand and was reading it with a frown. She couldn't think of anything else that would make him look so perplexed.

"When did this come?" His attention left the paper and focused on her. "This isn't my original release from the GPC. It's dated—" he looked down again "—three days ago. Why didn't you give me this? And why didn't they send it directly to me, like usual?"

She licked her dry lips. "Because Cantwell wasn't here yet, I guess. He was all scheduled to come, which is why they sent your papers, but then something went wrong, I don't know what." Except she did know. Colleen hadn't arranged for Cantwell's travel because a certain desperate, deceiving hospital director had lied and told her Trent had agreed to stay until the Gilchrist rep came.

The end justified the means, she tried to remind herself as she stared at the confusion on Trent's face. Except it was getting harder and harder to feel convinced of that.

"You still should have given them to me. Once the GPC releases me, my vacation is supposed to officially start. I need to find out when I'm expected in the Philippines now. That might have changed."

Her heart in her throat, she forced a smile. "I'm sorry if I messed this up. I'll call Colleen."

"Don't worry about it. I'll call."

His face relaxed into that charming smile of his, which somehow made the nervous twist in her stomach tighten even more painfully. The man really did like and trust her. Thank heavens the Gilchrist rep was due here any day, then this would all be over and he could be on his way.

And that thought made her stomach twist around and her chest ache in a whole different way.

"I've got my files here, Charlie. So I'm going to hit the road."

She turned to her dad, having nearly forgotten—again—that he was in the room. How was that possible since he stood only three feet from her? His expression was serious, speculative. Probably he, too, was wondering what was going on with her and why she'd buried Trent's papers deep within a pile.

"It's been nice to meet you, sir," Trent said, reaching to shake her dad's hand. "And don't worry. I'll take care of your daughter until I leave here."

"Thank you. I appreciate it."

"I'm standing right here, remember?" Relieved to be back to a joking mood, Charlie waved her hands. "How many times do I have to tell you two? I don't need to be taken care of."

"We know." Her dad smiled, but his eyes still

held a peculiar expression as he looked at her. "We just like to look after you. Is that so bad?"

She looked at Trent, horrified at the thought that filled her head. That she couldn't think of anything better than for him to stay here a full year, living with her and looking after her, the two of them looking after each other.

She could only imagine how appalled he'd be if he somehow read those thoughts in her face and she looked down at her desk as she changed the subject. "Can I help you get your things together, Dad? I'm about to head to the house anyway."

"Already done. My car's outside, ready to go." He pulled her into his arms for a hug. "We'll see you when you come visit next month."

"Can't wait to see both of you. Bye, Dad."

With a smile and a squeeze of Trent's hand, he disappeared, leaving the two of them alone in a room that now seemed no larger than a broom closet. She felt the heat of Trent's gaze on her, felt the electric zing from the top of her head to her toes, and slowly turned to look at him.

His hand reached out and swung the door closed, and that gesture, along with the look in his eyes as they met hers, made her heart beat hard at the same time as her stomach plunged.

She was crazy about this man. There was no getting around it, and she wanted so much to enjoy every last day, every last hour, every last minute she had with him. Surely he wouldn't find out about her lies? Maybe, even, he'd decide to stay longer on his own. It could happen, couldn't it?

She stepped forward at the same moment he did, their arms coming around one another, their lips fusing in a burning kiss that held a promise of tonight, at least, being one she'd never forget.

His warm palms slid slowly over her back, down her hips and back up, her body vibrating at his touch. The kiss deepened, his fingers pressed more urgently into her flesh and, when he broke the kiss, a little sound of protest left her tingling lips.

"You sure your desk is a little too small?" His eyes gleamed hotly, but still held that touch of humor she loved.

"Yes. We already had files all over the floor once tonight." The thought of why exactly that had happened took the pleasure of the moment down a notch, but she shook it off. She wasn't going to let anything ruin what could be one of her last nights with him. Reluctantly, she untangled herself from the warmth of his arms. "I'm going to head home. Join me for dinner about seven?"

"I'll be there." He leaned in once more, touched his lips to hers and held them there in a sweet and intimate connection that pinched her heart. "Don't be surprised if I'm even a little early."

She watched him leave, gripping the edge of her desk to hold herself upright, refusing to think about how, for the first time since she'd moved here, she would feel very lonely when he was gone.

The lowering sun cast shadows through the trees as Charlie approached her house, surprised to see Patience in front of the porch with little Lucky jumping around her feet.

"What are you doing here, Patience? Where's your dad?"

The little girl's smile faded into guilt. "Daddy was in a long, long meeting with Miss Mariam and I got tired of waiting. I came to show you the new trick I taught Lucky."

Oh, dear. John Adams was not going to be happy about this. "You know you're not allowed to leave the school and come all the way down here by yourself."

"I know. But it's just for a little bit. So I can show you. Then will you take me home?"

Charlie sighed. The child had the art of cajoling and wheedling down to a science. So much for getting showered and primped up before Trent came for their big date-night. "Okay. But promise me you won't do this again. You're not big enough to be running around all by yourself."

"I promise." The words came out grudgingly, but when Lucky yapped her eyes brightened again. "So, look! Sit, Lucky. Sit!"

The little pup actually did and Patience gave her some morsel as a reward, beaming with triumph as the dog began yapping and dancing again. "See Miss Charlie? She's really smart!"

"She is." She clapped her hands in applause, smiling at how cute and excited the child was. "And you being a good dog trainer helps her be smart."

"I know. I—"

A long, low growl behind her made Charlotte freeze, every hair on her scalp standing up in an instinctive reaction to the terrifying sound. She swung around and, to her horror, a large, feral and very angry dog stood there, its own hackles rising high on its back.

CHAPTER FIFTEEN

"PATIENCE." THE HARD hammering of her heart in her chest and her breath coming in short gasps made it difficult to sound calm. But the last thing she needed was for Patience to panic and make the situation worse. "Move very, very slowly and pick up Lucky, then quietly go up the porch steps and into the house. Don't make any sudden movements."

The child didn't say a word, probably as terrified as Charlie felt. The dog's lips were curled back in a snarl, showing every sharp tooth in its foamy mouth, and its jaws snapped together as it stared right at her. She couldn't risk turning around to see if Patience had done as she'd asked, because if it attacked she had to be ready. And it looked like it was about to do exactly that.

She glanced around for some weapon she could use to bash the dog if she had to. A sturdy stick was lying about five feet away and she slowly, carefully, inch by inch, sidled in that direction, her heart leaping into her throat as the dog growled louder, drool dripping as it snapped its jaws at her again.

Damn, this was bad. The animal had to be rabid; there was no other explanation for its aggression. That thought brought a horrified realization that this was probably the animal that had attacked and killed Patience's other dog. It was unusual enough to see feral dogs here and she knew the likely reason this one was still around was because it was very, very sick.

The sound of her screen door closing was a relief, and she prayed that meant Patience was out of harm's way. Should she try to talk soothingly to the dog? Or yell and try to scare it? She didn't know, and the last thing she wanted to do was something that would trigger it to attack her.

Sweat prickled at every pore, and her breath came fast and shallow as she kept her slow progress toward the stick, never taking her eyes off the animal. She was close. So close now. But how to pick it up when she got there? A fast movement to grab it and swing hard if the dog lunged? Keep her actions slow and steady, so she could get the stick in her hand and maybe not have to use it at all if she could just get back to the porch and in the house?

With her heart beating so hard it was practically a roar in her ears, she leaned down slowly, slowly, keeping her movements tight and controlled as she closed her fingers around the stick.

In an instant, the dog leaped toward her, mouth open, fangs dripping, knocking her to the ground, its teeth sinking deep into the flesh of her arm as she held it up in futile defense.

A scream of panic, of primal terror, tore from her throat. She tried to swing the stick at the dog, screaming again, but her position on the ground left her without much power behind the blow, and she realized the animal's teeth were sinking even deeper.

Some instinct told her to freeze and not to try to pull her arm from the dog's mouth, that it would just hold on tighter, shake her and injure her even worse. Its eyes were less than a foot from hers, wild eyes filled with fury above the jaws clamped onto her arm. It was so strong, so vicious, and a terrible helplessness came over her as she frantically tried to think how she could get away without getting hurt even worse, or maybe even being killed.

A loud, piercing gunshot echoed in the air and a split-second later the dog's jaws released her, its body falling limply on top of hers. Unable to process exactly what had happened, she grabbed her bleeding arm and tried to squirm out from under the beast.

"Charlotte." Trent was there, right there, his foot heaving the lifeless dog off her, crouching down beside her. "Damn it, Charlotte. Let me see."

"Trent." Her voice came out as a croak. It was Trent. Trent carefully holding her arm within his cool hands, looking down at it. Trent who had saved her life.

Her head dropped to the ground and she closed her eyes, saying a deep prayer of thanks as she began to absorb everything. Began to realize that the danger was past.

"Charlotte. Look at me." His gentle hand stroked her hair from her forehead and cupped her jaw, his thumb rubbing across her cheekbone. "Let me see." He tugged at her wrist and she realized she was still clutching her arm. She loosened her grip, feeling the sticky wetness of her blood on her hand as she dropped it to the ground. "You feel faint?"

"Y...yes." Stars sparkled in front of her eyes as she stared at the jagged gashes. At the oozing blood.

"Hang in there with me, sweetheart." He looked only briefly at her wounds before he yanked his shirt open—a nice, white button-down shirt, she processed vaguely—and quickly took it off. He wrapped it around her arm and applied a gentle pressure then lifted her hand up and placed it where his had been. "Squeeze to help stop the bleeding. I'm getting you to the clinic."

She could barely do as he asked but she tried. The screen door slammed behind them and Charlie became aware of the sound of Patience crying.

"Mr. Trent! Is Miss Charlie okay?"

"She's okay, but I need to take care of her. You stay in the house and I'll call your dad to come get you."

"O...okay."

The door slammed again as Trent lifted Charlie into his arms and strode in the direction of the hospital. She let her head loll against his muscled, bare shoulder, at the same time thinking she shouldn't let him haul her all the way there. She might not be big, but she wasn't a featherweight either.

"It's too far for you to carry me. I can walk."

"Like hell. For once, will you let someone take care of you? Let yourself off the hook for being in charge of the world?"

"I don't...I don't think I do that. But I admit I'm feeling a little shaky."

He looked down at her, his blue eyes somehow blazingly angry and tender at the same time. "A little shaky? You were just mauled by a rabid dog. You've lost a lot of blood. It's okay for you to lean on me a little, just once."

"Yes, doctor."

He gave her a glimmer of a smile. "Now that's what I like to hear. Keep pressing on your arm," he said as they finally got to the hospital and he laid her on an exam table. He placed a pillow beneath her head then made a quick call to John Adams. She watched him pull the pistol from his waistband and place it on the counter, wash his hands, then move efficiently to various cupboards, stacking things on the metal table next to her.

"Thank you. I...don't want to think about what might have happened if you hadn't come when you did."

"I don't want to think about it either." His

lips were pressed together in a grim line, his eyes stark as they met hers. "When I heard you scream, my heart about stopped."

"Why did you have a gun with you?"

"I work in plenty of unsafe places in the world, and always pack my thirty-eight. I had it with me because you left yours upstairs last time when you were supposed to be ready for a burglar, remember?"

She thought of how the dog had been right on top of her and shuddered. "How did you learn to shoot like that? Weren't you afraid you'd hit me instead?"

"No. Even though I was scared to death, I knew I'd hit the dog and not you." A tiny smile touched his lips as he placed items on the table. "I was on the trap and skeet shooting team at Yale. Rich boys get to have fun hobbies, and this one paid off."

Rich boys? She was about to ask, but he handed her a cup of water and several tablets. "What is this?"

"Penicillin. And a narcotic and fever-reducing combo. It'll help with the pain. I have to wash out your wounds, which is not going to feel good."

He lifted up her arm, placed a square plastic

bowl beneath it and began to unwrap his poor white shirt from it, now soaked in blood. Those little stars danced in front of her eyes again and she looked away. "Tell me the truth. How bad is it?"

"Bad enough. I'll know more in a few minutes." His expression was grim. "Because that dog was obviously rabid, I have to inject immunoglobulin. I'm also going to inject lidocaine because—"

"I know, I know. So I won't feel every stitch. Do it quick, please, and get it over with."

He gave a short laugh, shaking his head. "You're something else." He pressed a kiss to her forehead, before his eyes met hers, all traces of amusement gone. "Ready? This is going to hurt like hell. Hang in there for me."

She nodded and steeled herself, ashamed that she cried out at the first injection. "Sorry," she said, biting her lip hard. "I'm being a baby."

"No, you're not. I've seen big tough guys cry at this. You're awesome. Just a little longer."

When it was finally over, she could tell he felt as relieved as she did. "That's my girl." He pressed another lingering kiss to her head. "This next part is going to hurt, too, but not nearly as bad as that."

He poured what seemed like gallons of saline over her arm. He was right; it did not feel good. She thought he'd finally finished until he grabbed and opened another bottle. "Geez, enough already! What could possibly still be in there?"

"Is there some reason you have to keep questioning the doctor?" His blue eyes crinkled at the corners. "With all the technology and great drugs we have, thoroughly washing wounds like this—any animal bite, but especially when the dog is rabid—is the best treatment there is. But this is the last jug, I promise."

"Thank goodness. I was about to accuse you of making it hurt as much as you possibly can."

"And here I'd been giving you credit for being the bravest patient ever." His smile faded and he gave her a gentle kiss, his eyes tender. "I'm really sorry it hurts. Good news is, it looks like there's no arterial damage and the bites didn't go all the way to the bone. I'm going to throw some absorbable stitches into the deep muscle tears to control the bleeding then get everything closed up."

Instead of watching him work on her arm, she looked at his face. At the way his brows knit as he worked. At the way his dark lashes fanned over the deep focus of his eyes. At the way he sometimes pursed his lips as he stitched. Almost of its own accord, her hand lifted to cup his jaw and he paused to look at her, his blue eyes serious before he turned his face to her palm, pressing a lingering kiss there.

"Are you going to use a bunch of tiny stitches so I don't have awful scars?"

"I can't this round, sweetheart." He shook his head. "This kind of wound has a high risk for infection. We have to get the skin closed with as few stitches as possible, because the more I put in the more chance of infection. After it's healed completely, though, I can repair it so it looks better."

Except he wouldn't be here then. Their eyes met as the thought obviously came to both of them at the same time.

"I mean, one of your plastic surgeons can when the new wing is opened." His voice was suddenly brusque instead of sweet and tender.

She nodded and looked down, silently watching him work, her heart squeezing a little. How had she let herself feel this close to him? So close she would miss him far too much when he was gone.

When it was all over and her arm was wrapped in Kerlix, taped and put in a sling, he expelled a deep breath. "How about we head to your house and get you settled and comfortable? I'll carry you."

"I really am okay to walk." She didn't trust herself not to reveal her thoughts and feelings if he carried her, folded against his chest. "I need to."

He looked at her a moment then sighed. "All right. So long as you let me hold you in case you get dizzy."

Trent held her close as they walked slowly toward the front porch of her house and she let herself lean against his strength. The dog's body was gone, thank goodness, though there were bloodstains in the dirt. John Adams must've taken care of it. She was glad she didn't have to look at it and remember its wild eyes; see again those teeth that had ripped her flesh and held her tight in their grip.

"I feel kind of bad for the dog," she said.

"You feel sorry for the dog?" He stared down at her, eyebrows raised.

"Rabies is a pretty horrible way to die, isn't it? You shooting it was the best way for it to go."

"Yeah. It's one hundred percent fatal after it's been contracted. It's a good thing we have the vaccine to keep you safe from the virus." He looked away, his voice rough when he spoke again. "After you get settled inside, I'll come out and rake up the dirt. Don't think you want to be looking at your own blood every time you come in and out of your house."

"No. I don't." She looked up him and marveled at his consideration. "Who knew you were Mister Thoughtful and not the full-of-yourself guy I was convinced you were?"

"I'm both thoughtful *and* full of myself—multifaceted that way."

His eyes held a touch of their usual amusement and as she laughed her chest filled with some emotion she refused to examine.

CHAPTER SIXTEEN

TRENT KNEW THE narcotics would have worn off and Charlotte would be in pain again this morning. He'd slipped from the bed and gone downstairs to make toast and coffee for her, wanting something in her stomach before he gave her more fever medication, and the narcotic, too, if she needed it.

When he came back to her room with a tray, he had to pause inside the doorway just to look at her. Her lush hair tumbled across the pillow, the sun streaking through the windows highlighting its bronze glow. Her lips were parted, her shoulder exposed as one thin strap of her pretty nightgown had slid down her bandaged arm, leaving the gown gaping so low, one pink nipple was partly visible on her round breast.

He deeply inhaled, a tumble of emotions pummeling his heart as he stared at her. To his shock, the foremost emotion wasn't sexual.

It was a deep sense of belonging. Of belonging with her.

He wanted to stay here with her. He wanted to wake up in her bed, in her arms, every morning. He wanted to see her, just like this, at the start of each and every day.

Her eyelids flickered and she opened her eyes and looked at him. She smiled, and that smile seemed to reach right inside of him, pull him farther into the room. Pull him closer to her.

He managed to speak past the tightness in his chest. "Good morning, Charlotte." He set the tray on her nightstand and perched himself on the side of the bed. He stroked her hair from her face, wrapped a thick strand around his finger. "How's the arm feeling?"

"Not so great." She rolled onto her back, her lips twisting.

He ran his finger down her cheek. "I figured that. I brought you some toast and coffee and more meds."

"Thank you." Her good arm lifted to him and her palm stroked his cheek. He wished he'd shaved already, so the bristles wouldn't abrade her delicate skin when he kissed her. "But all I want is the fever stuff. I can't spend the day all doped up. I want to know exactly what's happening."

He nodded. "If you decide you need it later, you can always take it then. Why don't you sit up and have a little bit to eat first." He started to stand, but her hand grabbed the front of his shirt and bunched it up as she tugged him toward her.

"I am hungry again. But not for food—for you."

"Charlotte." He wanted, more than anything, to make love with her. But she was in pain and the need to take care of her, to keep her arm still so she wouldn't be in worse pain, took precedence over everything. "You need to rest."

"I've been resting all night. I slept very well, thanks to the drugs you gave me." She smiled at him and pulled harder on his shirt, bringing him closer still, and he could feel his resolve weakening at the way she looked at him. It was as though she was eating him up with her eyes and he knew he wanted to eat her up for real. "I do need to feel better. And you're very, very good at making me feel better."

"Well, I am a doctor. Took the Hippocratic Oath that I'd do the best I could to help my patients heal." He smiled, too, and gave up resisting. He gave in to the desire spiraling through his body. "What can I do first to make you feel better?"

"Kiss me."

Her tongue flicked across her lips and he leaned forward to taste them, carefully keeping his body from resting against her arm. It took every ounce of self-control to keep himself in check, to touch her and kiss her slowly, carefully.

"Does it make you feel better if I do this?" He gently drew her nightgown down and over her bandages, then lifted her arm carefully above her head to rest it on her pillow. He traced the tops of her breasts with his fingertips, slowly, inching across the soft mounds, until he pulled the lacy nightgown down to fully expose her breasts.

The sunlight skimmed across the pink tips and his breath clogged in his throat as he enjoyed the incredible beauty of them. Of her. He lowered his mouth to one nipple then rolled it beneath his tongue, drew it into his mouth and lifted his hand to cup the other breast in his palm.

"Yes," she murmured. The hand on her good arm rested on the back of his head, her fingers tangling in his hair. "I'm feeling better already."

"How about this?" His mouth replaced his hand on her other breast, his fingertips stroking along her collarbone, her armpit, down her ribs, and he reveled in the way she shivered in response.

"Yes. Good."

He slowly tugged her nightgown farther down her body, gently touching every inch he could with his mouth, his tongue, his hands. He could feel her flesh quiver, felt the heat pumping from her skin, and marveled at how excruciatingly pleasurable it was to take it this slow. To think only of making her feel good, to feel wonderful, to feel loved.

The shocking thought made him freeze and raise his head.

Loved? He didn't do love.

But as he looked down at her eyes, at the softness, heat and desire in their green depths, his heart squeezed at the same time it expanded.

He did love her. He loved everything about her. He loved her sweetness, her toughness and her stubbornness and was shocked all over again. Shocked that the realization didn't scare the crap out of him. Shocked that, instead, it filled him with wonder.

He lowered his mouth to hers, drinking in the taste of her, and for a long, exquisite moment there was only that simple connection. His lips to hers, hers to his, and through the kiss he felt their hearts and souls connecting as well.

He drew back, and saw the reflection of what he was feeling in her eyes. Humbled and awed, he smiled. "Still feeling good? Or do you need a little more doctoring?"

"More please." She returned his smile, which changed to a gasp when he slipped his hand beneath her nightgown, found her moist core and caressed it.

"We need to lose this gown. I want to see all of you. Touch and kiss all of you." He dragged the gown to her navel, her hipbones, his mouth and tongue following the trail along her skin. He wanted nothing more than this. He wanted to help her forget her pain. For her to feel only pleasure.

She lifted her bottom to help him pull it all the way off, and he took advantage of the arch of her hips, kissing her there, touching and licking the velvety folds until she was writhing beneath his mouth.

"Trent," she gasped. "You've proven how good you are at making me feel better. But I want more. Why are you still dressed? I don't think I can strip you with only one hand."

He looked at her and had to grin at the desire and frustration on her face. "You want me to strip? I'm at your command, boss lady." He quickly shucked his clothes and took one more moment to take in the beauty of her nakedness, before carefully positioning himself on top of her as she welcomed him.

With her eyes locked on his, he moved within her. Slowly. Carefully. She met him, moved beneath him, urged him on. The sounds of pleasure she made nearly undid him and he couldn't control the ever-faster pace. There was nothing more important in the world than this moment, this rhythm that was unique to just the two of them, joining as one. And, when she cried out, he lost himself in her.

Curled up with Trent's body warming her back, his arms holding her close, Charlie felt sated, basking in the magic of being with him; wanting to know more about him.

"Tell me about being a rich boy. That's what you said you are, isn't it?"

He didn't respond for a moment then a soft sigh tickled her ear. "Yes. My family is wealthy and I have a trust fund that earns more money each year than most people make in ten."

"And yet you work in mission hospitals all over the world. Why?"

"For the same reason you live and work here— to give medical care to those who wouldn't have any if we didn't."

She turned her head to try to look at his face. "When did you decide to live your life that way instead of working in some hospital in the States? Or being a plastic surgeon for the rich and famous?"

The laugh he gave didn't sound like there was much humor in it. "Funny you say that. My dad and grandfather have exactly that kind of practice. I was expected to follow in their footsteps, but realized I didn't want to. When I was about two-thirds of the way through my plastics residency, I knew I wanted to do a surgical fellowship in pediatric neurosurgery instead."

Wow. She'd known he had amazing skills, but he did brain surgery too? "Did you?"

"No. I couldn't get into a program. Was rejected by every one I applied to. Then found out why."

She waited for him to continue but he didn't. "So, why?"

He didn't speak for a long time. She was just about to turn in his arms, to look in his eyes and see what was going on with him, when he answered. His voice was grim. "My mother was hell-bent on me joining the family practice. I didn't realize how hell-bent until I found out she'd used her family name, wealth and the power behind all of that to keep me out of any neurosurgery program. All the while pretending she supported my decision, when in fact she was manipulating the outcome. So I left. Left the country to do mission work, and I haven't been back since."

Charlie's breath backed up in her lungs and her heart about stopped. His mother had deceived him and lied? He'd obviously been horribly hurt by it. So hurt that he'd cut his family from his life. So hurt that he'd left the U.S. and hadn't returned.

It also sounded horrifyingly similar to what she'd been doing to him, too.

Her stomach felt like a ball of lead was weighing it down. "I'm…sorry you had such a difficult time and that you were hurt by all that."

"Don't be. It's ancient history, and it was good I learned what kind of person she really is."

The lead ball grew heavier at his words, making her feel a little sick, and she couldn't think of a thing to say. He kissed her cheek, his lips lingering there, and a lump formed in her throat at the sweetness of the touch.

"I'm going to fix you some brunch. Something better than the toast you didn't eat." He nipped lightly at her chin, her lips. "And, just for you, I'm going to perform a surgery today that I think will make you happy. But I'm not telling until after it's done."

She squeezed his hand and tried to smile. "Can't wait to hear about it." She drew in a breath and shook off her fears. He wouldn't find out. It would be okay. They'd get the donation check, the new wing would open and, when all that was behind them…then what?

She knew, and her heart swelled in anticipation. She'd ask him to stay, and not for the hospital. She'd tell him she was crazy about him, that she wanted to see where their relationship could go. The thought scared her and thrilled her; she was not sure how risky that would be. How it would feel to share her life and her world with someone. But she knew, without question, it was a risk she had to take.

By the way he'd made love to her, looked at her, taken care of her, maybe he'd actually say yes.

CHAPTER SEVENTEEN

TRENT LEFT THE OR, feeling damned pleased at the way the cleft palate surgery had gone for the child. He knew Charlotte would be happy too and couldn't wait to tell her.

The satisfaction he felt made him realize he'd been too hasty believing the skills he had were superfluous and not a good way to help people, and children in particular, as he wanted to. Working in his family's cosmetic surgery practice hadn't been what he wanted. But Charlotte had helped him see that those skills really were valuable in helping people have better lives.

While he'd done plastics procedures at many of his other jobs, it had taken her dogged persistence to make him see how important those techniques could be to those without hope of improving their lives that way except through a hospital like this one.

Striding down the hall, he couldn't believe his eyes, seeing the woman who was on his mind.

There she stood, talking to John Adams, like it had been a week instead of a day since her ordeal. Hadn't he specifically told her to stay home and rest?

"What possible excuse do you have for being here, Charlotte?"

"I got bored. There's too much to do to just sit around."

"You're not just sitting around." He wanted to shake the damn stubborn woman. "Resting helps your body heal. Gives it a chance to fight infection. Which, in case you don't remember, is particularly important after a nasty dog bite." He turned to John Adams. "Can you talk sense into her?"

"Last time she listened to me was about six months ago or so," he replied, shaking his head.

Trent turned back to her, more than ready to get tough if he had to. "Don't make me drag you back there and tie you down."

She scowled then, apparently seeing that he was completely serious, gave a big, dramatic sigh. "Fine. I'll go rest some more. Though every hour feels like five. Can I at least take a few files with me to go over while I'm being quiet?"

The woman was unbelievable. "If you abso-

lutely have to. But no moving around unneces-
sarily. No cooking dinner. I'll take care of that."

"Yes, Dr. Dalton."

He ignored the sarcastic tone. "That's what I
want to hear from my model patient." He noted
the blue shadows beneath her eyes, the slight
tightness around her mouth that doubtless was
from pain she was determined not to show, and
couldn't help himself. He leaned down to give
her a gentle kiss, not caring that John Adams was
standing right there. "I just finished the cleft palate surgery I promised you I'd do. Now I want
you to give me a promise in return— that you'll
take care of yourself. For me, if not for yourself."

Her eyes softened at the same time they glowed
with excitement. "You fixed the boy's cleft palate
today? That's wonderful! Did you take pictures
like I asked you to? I need pictures to— Well, I
just think we should keep a record."

"All taken care of. Now for your promise."

"I promise." She sent him a smile so wide, it
lit the room. "I'll see you at home."

At home. That had a nice sound to it. He found
himself admiring her shapely legs beneath her
skirt, watching the slight sway of her hips all the
way down the hall and out the door, and when

he turned he saw John Adams eyeing him speculatively.

"So, is something going on between you and Charlie? I thought you were leaving in just a day or two. Speaking of which, did you go over everything Thomas needs to know about her stitches and the rabies vaccine course?"

He looked back at the door Charlotte had disappeared out of, and realized if he left it would be just like that—she'd disappear from his life and he'd likely never see her again.

With absolute conviction that it was the right decision, he knew he wasn't going to leave. He had to be here to take care of her, to improve the scarring on her arm after she was healed, to see exactly what a year with her would be like.

He turned back to John Adams. "I'm staying."

The man smiled and clapped him on the shoulder. "Good to hear. Welcome to the family."

Trent changed out of his scrubs, cleaned up and called Mike Hardy before going to Charlotte's so he could tell her his decision. He could only hope she'd be as happy about him staying as he felt about it. Thinking of the way they'd made love just that morning, the look on her face and in her beautiful eyes as they'd moved together, he had a pretty powerful feeling that she would be.

"Mike? Trent Dalton. How are you?"

"Good, Trent. Great to hear from you. Are you enjoying your vacation in Italy?"

"No." Had the man forgotten about all the delays? "I'm still at the Edwards Hospital in Liberia."

"You're still in Liberia?" The man sounded astonished. "Why? Perry Cantwell went there last week, so you should be long gone by now."

"Perry was delayed, so I had to stay on until he could get here." How could Mike not know all this? "I've decided I want to stay here for the next year. I'd like you to find a replacement for me in the Philippines and draw up a new contract for me."

"Trent, we never have two doctors at the Edwards Hospital. We just can't afford it."

He frowned. Mike usually bent over backwards if he had a special request, which he rarely did. Trent was one of only a handful of GPC docs that worked for them full-time, year-round. "I don't need another doc here with me. I'm sure Perry wouldn't care if he's here or in the Philippines. Ask him."

There was a silence on the line, which made Trent start to feel a little fidgety, until Mike finally spoke again. "I just found your file to see what's going on. Your release papers were sent well over a week ago. And I know Perry was about on his way when I had Colleen send them, so I'm confused. This is all a real problem, messing up your pay and vacation time and next assignment. I need to talk to Colleen and find out how these mistakes happened before we have any more discussion about you staying there. I'll call you back."

"All right."

The conversation with Mike left him feeling vaguely disturbed, but he brushed it off. He couldn't imagine there would be a problem. It probably would just come down to shuffling paperwork.

Since he had no idea when Mike would call him back, he went on to Charlotte's house. If he didn't find her resting, he was going to threaten her with something—maybe refusing to kiss her or make love with her would be a strong enough incentive, he thought with a smile. He knew that if she threatened him with something similar he'd follow any and all instructions.

He let himself in the door. Seeing her curled up in the armchair, her hair falling in waves around her shoulders, her expression relaxed, filled his chest with a sense of belonging that he couldn't remember having felt since before he'd left the States. Since before the betrayal by his mother. A cozy, welcoming old home with a beautiful and more than special woman inside waiting for him was something he'd never thought he wanted until now.

He stood there a moment, knowing he was beyond blessed to have been sent to this place on what was supposed to have been a fill-in position for just a few days. Another example of the universe guiding his life in ways he could never have foreseen.

"Hey, beautiful." He leaned down to kiss the top of her head, his lips lingering in the softness of her hair. "Thank you for being good, sitting there reading. I'm proud of you."

Her hand cupped his cheek, her eyes smiled up at him, and that feeling in his chest grew bigger, fuller. "I decided I should do what you ask, since you did that cleft palate surgery today like you promised. Not to mention that whole saving my life thing." Her voice grew softer. "I'm so lucky to have you here."

He was the lucky one. "I want you to eat so you can take some more pain medicine before that arm starts to really hurt again. Let me see what's in the kitchen."

His cell rang while he was putting a quick dinner together and he was glad it was Mike Hardy. "What'd you find out?"

"You're not going to like it." Mike's voice was grim and a sliver of unease slid down Trent's back. "Colleen's over here wringing her hands."

"Why?"

"She sent your release papers to the director of the hospital, instead of to you, because Charlotte Edwards asked her to. Apparently she's a good friend of Colleen's, and said she'd pass them on to you. Ms. Edwards also told her not to schedule Perry's travel yet because she claimed you'd agreed to stay on another two weeks.

"According to Colleen, the hospital has to have a plastic surgeon on site when the Gilchrist Foundation rep comes there in another day or so. If it doesn't, she won't get the donation she needs and won't be able to pay the bills. I guess they're pretty deep in the hole over there, might even have to shut the whole thing down. Charlotte Edwards's solution was to keep you there—get you to do some plastic surgeries she could impress Gilchrist with and pass you off as her new plastic surgeon. After that, Colleen was going to get Perry there and you could be on your way. But it's obvious you didn't know about any of this."

With every word Mike spoke, Trent's hands grew colder until he was practically shaking from the inside out with shock and anger. Everything Charlotte had said to him spun through his mind: praising his plastic surgery skills, begging him to do those surgeries and take photos, telling him there were problems with his paperwork, delays in getting Perry there. Coming up with a fake excuse when he'd found his release papers in her office.

Flat-out lying to him all along. Manipulating his papers, his life. His heart.

It was like *déjà vu*, except this was so much worse. Because she'd obviously only been pretending to like him. She'd obviously only had sex with him to keep him there, to tangle him up with her so he wouldn't leave until after the Gilchrist rep came.

And what had Mike said? After that, Colleen

had the green light to get him out of there. *Bye-bye, have a nice life, I don't need you anymore.*

How could he have been so stupid, so blind? It was all so clear now, all the plastic surgery crap lines she'd fed him.

She hadn't cared when he'd left the first time and she sure as hell wouldn't care this time.

Balling his hands into fists, he sucked in a heavy breath, trying to control the bottomless anger and pain that filled his soul until it felt like it just might rip apart.

He had to get out of there. He'd already gone over with Thomas what had to happen with the rabies vaccine. She'd be all right. And the fact that the thought came with a brief worry on her behalf made him want to punch himself in the face.

Fool me once, shame on you. Fool me twice, and I'm obviously a pathetic moron.

"Thanks for telling me, Mike. I'm going to make my own arrangements to leave."

"All right. Perry's travel arrangements are being finalized this minute, so he'll be there soon."

Somehow, he managed to finish fixing Charlotte's dinner while he dialed the airline, relieved to find he could be out of there at the crack of dawn tomorrow.

He set her food on the table, placed two pain tablets next to it and forced himself to go into the parlor. The smile she sent him across the room felt like a stab wound deep into his heart. "Dinner's on the table. Come eat, then take your pills."

As she passed through the kitchen doorway, he stepped back, not wanting to touch her. Knowing a touch would hurt like a bad burn, and he'd been scorched enough.

"Where's yours?" She looked at him in surprise, her pretty, lying lips parted.

He'd play the part she'd once accused him of, so she wouldn't know he knew the truth. So she wouldn't know how much it hurt that she'd used him. That the pain went all the way to the core of his very essence, leaving a gaping hole inside.

It seemed like a long time since she'd told him he was full of himself and famous for kissing women goodbye with a smile and a wave. He'd do it now if it killed him.

"Colleen Mason just called to tell me I have a plane reservation in the morning, that I've been given the all-clear," he said, somehow managing a fake smile.

She sank onto the kitchen chair, staring. "What? I don't understand. I don't have... Perry Cantwell's not...I mean, that can't be right."

"It is. My vacation's been delayed long enough, and I'm meeting a...friend...in Florence." He leaned down to brush his lips across hers, and was damned if the contact wasn't excruciating. "It's been great being with you. But you know how I feel about long goodbyes, so I'll get out of here."

"But, Trent. Wait. I—"

"Take care of that arm." He turned and moved quickly to the door, unable to look at her face. To see the shock and despair and, damn it, the tears in her eyes. To know her dismay had nothing to do with him and everything to do with her precious hospital.

The thought came to him that he was running again. Running from pain, disillusionment and deep disappointment. And this time he knew he just might be running for the rest of his life.

CHAPTER EIGHTEEN

CHARLIE LAID HER head on her desk because she didn't think she could hold it upright for one more minute.

In barely forty-eight hours, her life had gone to ruin, and no amount of hard work and positive attitude was going to fix it.

She'd been a fool to think there had been any possibility of her relationship with Trent Dalton becoming anything bigger than a fling. It'd been foolish to allow her feelings to get out of control. To allow the connection she felt to him to grab hold of her—a connection that had bloomed and deepened until she could no longer deny the emotion.

She thought she'd seen that he felt it too. Had seen it in his eyes; seen it in the way he cared for her when she'd been hurt; seen it through his kisses and his touch.

Then he'd walked out. One minute he was sweetly there, the next he was kissing her goodbye with a smile and a wave, just like the first time. But, unlike the first time, he'd taken a big chunk of her heart with him.

How could she have been so stupid? She'd known all along it could never be more than a fling. Had known he was right, when he'd come back, that they should keep their relationship platonic—because, as he'd so eloquently said, second goodbyes tended to get messy.

Messy? Was that the way to describe how he'd left? It seemed like their goodbye had been quite neat and tidy for him.

Anger burned in her stomach. Anger that she'd let herself fall for a man who'd never hidden that he didn't want or need roots. Anger that the pain of his leaving nagged at her far more than the physical pain of her torn and stitched-up arm.

And of course, practically the minute he'd moved on, the Gilchrist rep had shown up. He'd been impressed with the wing but, gosh, there was this little problem of there not being a doctor there. She'd hoped the photographs of Trent's work would help, but of course it hadn't. After all, the man was long gone, and they'd made their requirements very clear.

A quiet knock preceded the door opening and

Charlie managed to lift her head to look at John Adams, swallowing the lump that kept forming in her throat.

"I'm guessing things didn't go well," he said as he sat in the chair across from her.

"No. The Gilchrist Foundation can't justify giving us the check without meeting all their requirements. Which I knew would happen."

"What are you going to do?"

Wasn't that a good question? What was she going to do to keep the hospital open? What was she going to do to mend her broken heart? What was she going to do to move past the bitterness and regret that was like a burning hole in her chest?

"I don't know. I have to crunch the numbers again, see what can be eliminated from the budget. Lay off a few employees. See if any of the other donors I've approached will come through with something." Though nothing could come close to what Gilchrist had offered. To what the hospital needed.

"There is the money the anonymous donor gave the school." John Adams looked at her steadily. "I can put off hiring another teacher, hold off on some of the purchases we made."

"No." She shook her head even as the suggestion was tempting. "Whoever donated that money gave it to the school. It wouldn't be right to use it for the hospital. I'll figure something out."

"All right." John Adams stood and gently patted her head, as though she were Patience. "I'm sorry about all this. And sorry about Trent leaving. I've got to tell you, that surprised me. Especially since it was right after he'd told me he was staying."

"He told you he was staying?"

"He did. After he was irritated with you being in the hospital when you were supposed to be resting."

And his caring for her through all that was part of what had made her fall harder for him. "Well, he obviously didn't mean it the way most people would. Staying the night is probably what that word means to him." She tried to banish the acrid and hurt tone from her voice. After all, she'd known the reality. Regret yet again balled up in her stomach that she'd allowed herself to forget it.

Trent walked beneath the trees in Central Park to his parents' Fifth Avenue apartment on Manhattan's Upper East Side. He breathed in the scents of the city, listened to children playing in the park and the constant flow of traffic crowding the street and looked at the old and elegant apartment buildings that lined the streets.

It didn't seem all that many years ago since he'd been a kid roaming these streets, not realizing at the time how different growing up here was from the average kid's childhood in suburbia. But it had been great too, in its own way, especially when your family had wealth and privilege enough to take advantage of everything the city offered and the ability to leave for a quieter place when the hustle got wearying.

His mother had been more hands-on than most of the crowd his parents were friends with, whose full-time nannies did most of the child-rearing. He'd appreciated it, and how close they'd been, believing that the bond she shared with her only child was special to her.

Until she'd lied and betrayed him. The memory of that blow still had the power to hurt.

He thought of how his mother had tried to reach out to him during the years since then. She'd kept tabs on wherever he was working, and each time he moved on to a new mission hospital a Gilchrist Foundation donation immediately plumped their coffers. She'd sent him a Christmas card every year, with updates on what she and his dad were doing, where they'd traveled, asking questions about his own life. Questions he hadn't answered. After all, what he wanted to do with his life hadn't interested her before, so he figured it didn't truly interest her now.

She'd been shocked and seemingly thrilled to get his phone call that morning and he wondered what it would be like to see her after all this time. A part of him dreaded it. The part of him that still carried good memories wanted, in spite of everything, to see how she was. Either way, the need at the Edwards hospital was what had driven him here. Not for Charlotte—for all the patients who would have nowhere to go if the place shut down.

"Mr. Trent! Is that you? I can't believe it!" Walter Johnson pumped his hand, a broad smile on the old doorman's face.

"Glad to see you're still here, Walter." Trent smiled, thinking of all the times the man had had his back when he'd been a kid. "It's been a long time since my friends and I were causing trouble for you."

"You just caused normal boy trouble. Kept my

job interesting." Walter grinned. "Are your parents expecting you? Or shall I ring them?"

"My mother knows I'm coming. Thanks."

The ornate golden elevator took him to his family's fourteen-room apartment and he drew a bracing breath before he knocked on the door. Would she look the same as always? Or would time have changed her some?

The door opened and his question was answered. She looked lovely, like she always had. Virtually unchanged—which wasn't surprising, considering his dad was a plastic surgeon and there were all kinds of cosmeceuticals out there now to keep wrinkles at bay. Her ash-blonde hair was stylishly cut and she wore her usual casual-chic clothes that cost more than most of his patients made in a year.

"Trent!" She stepped forward and he thought she was going to throw her arms around him, but she hesitated, then grasped his arm and squeezed. "It's just…wonderful to see you. Come in. Tell me about yourself and your life and everything."

Sunlight pouring through the sheer curtains cast a warm glow upon the cream-colored, modern furnishings in the room as they sat in two chairs at right angles to one another. One of her housekeepers brought coffee and the kind of biscuits Trent had always liked, and he felt a little twist of something in his chest that she had remembered.

"My life is good." Okay, that was a lie, right off the bat. His life was absolute crap and had been ever since he'd found out Charlotte had lied to him, that their relationship had been, for her at least, a means to an end and nothing more.

For the first time in his life, he'd fallen hard for a woman. A woman who was like no one he'd ever met before. Had finally realized, admitted to himself, that what he felt for Charlotte went far beyond simple attraction, lust or friendship with benefits.

And, just as he'd been ready to find out exactly what all those feelings were and what they meant, he'd been knocked to the ground by the truth and had no idea how he was going to get back up again.

"We've...we've missed you horribly, Trent." His mother twisted her fingers and stared at him through blue eyes the same color as his own. "I know you were angry when you left and I understand why. I understand that I was wrong to do what I did and I want to explain."

"Frankly, Mom, I don't think any explanation could be good enough." He didn't want to hash it out all over again. It was history and he'd moved on. "I'm not here to talk about that. I'm here to ask you a favor."

"Anything." She placed her hand on his knee. "What is it?"

"I've been working at the Edwards hospital in Liberia. They'd applied to you, to the Gilchrist Foundation, for a large donation to build and open a plastic surgery wing."

She nodded. "Yes. I'm familiar with it. In fact, I just received word that we won't be providing the donation now because they didn't meet the criteria."

"They're doing good work, Mom, and use their money wisely. I performed some plastic surgeries there and saw how great the need is. I'd appreciate it if you would still give them the donation."

"You did plastic surgery there?" She looked surprised. "Last time I spoke with you, when you stormed out of here, you told me that wasn't what you wanted to do. What changed your mind?"

"I haven't changed my mind. I didn't want to join the family practice doing facelifts and breast implants. I wanted to use my surgical skills to help children. But I've realized that I can do both."

"Are you working at the Edwards hospital full-time now? Permanently?"

"No." He'd never go there again, see Charlotte Edwards again. "It was time to leave. But I know they're getting a surgeon as soon as they can. I'd appreciate you giving them the funding check, which will help the rest of the hospital too. The people there need it."

"All right, if it's important to you, I'll get it wired out tomorrow."

"Thank you. I'm happy that, this time, what's important to me matters to you." Damn it, why had that stupid comment come out of his mouth? She'd agreed to do as he asked. The last thing he wanted was for her to change her mind, or dredge up their past.

"Trent." He looked at her, and his gut clenched at the tears that swam in her eyes. "Anything that's important to you is important to me. I know you don't want to hear it, but I'm telling you any-way—why I did what I did." She grabbed one of the tiny napkins that had been served with the coffee and dabbed her eyes. "When I went to col-lege, all I wanted was to be a doctor. To become a plastic surgeon like my father and join his practice. I studied hard in college, and when I applied to medical schools I got in. But my father said no. Women didn't make good doctors, he said, and especially not good surgeons. I couldn't be a wife and mother and a surgeon too and needed to understand my place in our social strata."

He stared at her, stunned. It didn't surprise him that his autocratic grandfather could be such a son-of-a-bitch. But his mother wanting to be a doctor? He couldn't wrap his brain around it. "I don't know what to say, Mom. I had no idea."

"So I married your dad and he joined the practice. Filled my life with my philanthropy, which has been rewarding. And with you. You were… are…the most important thing in my life. Until I messed everything up between us." The tears filled her eyes again and he was damned if they didn't send him reaching to squeeze her shoulder, pat her in comfort, in spite of everything.

"It's all right, Mom. It was a long time ago."

"I want you to understand why, even though there's no excuse, and I know that now." Her hand reached to grip his. "I just wanted you to have what I couldn't have. I wanted that for you, and couldn't see, because of my own disappointment from all those years ago, that it was for me and not for you. That I was being selfish, instead of caring. I'm so very, very sorry and I hope someday you can forgive me. All I ever wanted was for you to be happy. You may not believe that, but it's true."

He looked at her familiar face, so full of pain and sadness. The face of the person who had been the steadiest rock throughout his life, until the moment she wasn't.

He thought about the fun they'd had when he was growing up, their adventures together, her sense of humor. He thought about how she'd always been there for him, and for his friends too, when most of their parents weren't around much. And he thought about how much he'd loved her and realized that hadn't changed, despite the anger he'd felt and the physical distance between them for so long.

He thought of how many times she'd tried to reach out to him through the cards she sent and through giving to the places he worked, places that were important to him.

As he stared into her blue eyes, he knew it was time to reach back.

"I do believe it, Mom. I'm sorry too. Sorry I let

so many years go by before I came home. I don't completely understand, but I do forgive you. Let's put it all behind us now." He leaned forward to hug her and she clung to him, tears now stream-ing down her face.

"Okay. Good." She pulled back, dabbing her face with the stupid little napkin, and smiled through her tears. "So I have a question for you."

"Ask away."

"Are you in love with the woman in charge of the Edwards hospital?"

He stared at her in shock. She had on her "mom" look he'd seen so many times in his life. The one that showed she knew something he didn't want her to know. He was damned if the woman hadn't always had a keen eye and a sixth sense when it came to her only child. "Why would you ask that?"

"Because you've been working in hospitals all over the world for years, and I know you donate money to them. There must be some reason you came here to see me and ask me to give the Ed-wards hospital the foundation money, and some reason you're not donating your own." She arched her brows. "If she hurt you, I'm taking back my agreement to give them the money."

He shook his head, nearly chuckling at her words, except the pain he felt over Charlotte's lies was too raw. "She worked hard to get the Gilchrist Foundation donation. I'd like it to come through for her and the hospital."

"And?"

He sighed. Sitting here with her as she prodded him for information felt like the years hadn't passed and he was a teenager again. "Yes, I'm in love with her. No, she doesn't return my feelings." Saying it brought to the surface the pain he was trying hard to shove down.

"How do you know? Did she tell you that?"

"She lied to me and used me. Tried to keep me there just to get your donation for her precious hospital. Not something someone does to someone they love."

"I don't know. I love you but I lied and made stupid mistakes. Have you told her how you feel?"

He stared at her, considering her words. Could Charlotte have done what she did and still cared about him at the same time? "No. And I'm not going to."

"But you still love her enough to make sure she gets the donation from my foundation."

"It's for the hospital, not her." But as he said

the words he knew it was for Charlotte as well, and hated himself for it.

She regarded him steadily. "I think it's for both the hospital *and* her. I made a bad mistake. Maybe she did too. Don't compound it by making your own mistakes." She stood and smiled, holding out her hand like he was still a little kid. "Come on, prodigal son. Your dad will be home soon. Stay for dinner and we'll catch up."

"I'm sorry, Colleen. For everything. I hope Mike wasn't mad that you sent the release papers to me instead of Trent." Charlie studied her online bank statements as she talked to her friend, despairing that she'd find a way out of their financial problems. With everything else a total mess, getting Colleen in trouble would make the disaster complete.

"No, he's not. I wish you hadn't lied to me, though."

"I know. I'm so, so sorry. Everything I did was stupid and didn't even solve anything."

"I bet Trent was really angry about it." Her voice was somber. "I know he left there—I arranged his travel for when he heads to Europe from the U.S. What did he say?"

"He never found out, thank heavens." That would have been the worst thing of all. Despite the crappy way he'd left, she wouldn't have wanted him to know what she'd done.

"What do you mean? Of course he did. He was telling Mike he wanted to stay there in Liberia. Be assigned at your hospital for the year. And that's when Mike told him everything you'd done."

Charlie's heart lurched then seemed to grind to a halt. The world felt a little like it was tilting on its axis, and as she stared, unseeing, at her office wall, it suddenly became horribly, painfully clear.

Trent hadn't left because he was tired of her, ready for vacation, ready to move on. He'd left because he knew she'd lied and manipulated his paperwork. He'd left because of what she'd done to him.

"Oh my God, Colleen," she whispered. Trent had once told her that trying to control the direction the world spun would end up weighing heavily on her shoulders. Little had he known exactly how true that was. At this moment, that weight felt heavy indeed.

Numb, she absently noted a ping on her computer that showed a wire transfer from a bank.

Mind reeling, she forced herself to focus on business. Any money would help pay a bill or two.

But when she pulled it up, her mind reeled even more dizzily. Air backed up in her lungs and she couldn't breathe. "Oh my God," she said again, but this time it was different. This time it was in stunned amazement. "It's the donation from the Gilchrist Foundation. All of it they'd committed to us. What…? Why…this is unbelievable!"

"Oh, Charlie, I'm so happy for you! This is awesome!"

"Yes. It is. Listen, I need to go. I'll call you later." Charlie hung up and stared at the wire transfer, unable to process that it had come through, beyond relieved that the hospital wouldn't have to shut down. Once the plastic surgeon showed, they'd be able to get the wing open and operating for a long time, helping all those who so needed it.

But knowing her project would now be complete didn't bring the utter satisfaction it should have. Didn't feel like the epitome of everything she'd wanted. And as she stared at her computer she knew why.

She'd ruined the sweet, wonderful, fledging romance that had blossomed between her and

Trent. Through her adamant "the end justifies the means" selfish attitude, she'd no doubt hurt the most amazing, giving, incredible man she'd ever known.

He'd wanted to stay the year with her, which just might have turned into forever. But instead, she'd destroyed any chance of happiness, of a real relationship with him.

Her computer screen blurred as tears filled her eyes and spilled down her cheeks. How could she have been so stubbornly focused on the hospital's future that she couldn't see her own, staring her in the face through beautiful blue eyes?

She'd always prided herself on being a risk-taker. But when it came to the most important risk of all—risking her emotions, her life and her heart—she'd cowardly backed away in self-protection. Afraid to expose herself to potential pain, she'd tried to close a shell around her heart, hiding inside it like a clam. But somehow he'd broken through that shell anyway.

Why hadn't she seen she should have been honest with Trent, and with herself, about all of it? Maybe the outcome would have been different if she had, but now she'd never know. Trent doubtless hated her now, and she had only herself to blame.

Her phone rang, and she blinked at the tears stinging her eyes, swallowing down the lump in her throat to answer it. "Charlotte Edwards here."

"Ms. Edwards, this is Catherine Gilchrist Dalton. I'm founder and president of the Gilchrist Foundation. I wanted to make sure you received our donation via wire."

"Yes, I did, just now." The woman was calling her personally? "I'm honored to speak with you and more than honored to receive your donation. I appreciate it more than I can possibly say, and I promise to use it wisely."

"As you know, your hospital was originally denied because it didn't meet our requirements."

"Yes. I know." And she hoped the woman would tell her why they'd changed their minds, though she supposed it didn't really matter.

"My son, Trent Dalton—I think you know him?—he came to see me, asking me to still provide the donation. Convinced me your hospital is more than worthy of our funding."

Charlotte nearly dropped her phone. Trent? Trent was the woman's son? She tried to move her lips, but couldn't speak.

"Hello? Are you there?"

"Y…yes. I'm sorry. I'm just…surprised to hear that Trent is your son." Surprised didn't begin to cover it. He'd called himself a rich boy? That was an understatement.

"Perhaps I'm being a busybody, but that's a mother's prerogative. Trent told me he'd wanted to spend the next year working at your hospital with you, but you made a mistake by lying to him which has made him change his mind."

"Yes, that's true." Her voice wobbled. "I was selfishly stupid and would give anything to be able to do it over again. To be honest with him about…everything."

"Would that 'everything' include caring for him in a personal way? Being his mother, I would have to assume you do."

The woman's amused tone reminded her so much of Trent, she nearly burst into tears right into the phone. "You're right, Mrs. Dalton. I do care for Trent in a personal way, because he's the most incredible man I've ever known. I'm terribly, crazy in love with him but, if he cared at all about me before, I don't think he does anymore. I don't think he'll ever forgive me."

"You won't know unless you try to find out,

will you? I made a terrible mistake with him once, too, tried to manipulate his life and paid a harsh price for that. Our years of separation were very painful to me, and I should have tried harder to apologize, to ask him to forgive me. I suggest you make the effort, instead of wondering. And maybe regretting."

She was right. A surge of adrenaline pulsed through Charlie's blood. She'd find Trent and she'd make it right or die trying. "Thank you. Do you know where he is?"

"He's here in New York City, visiting with a few friends. He's leaving soon. I can try to find out his travel plans, if you like."

Colleen. Colleen had his itinerary. "Thanks, but I think I know how to get them."

CHAPTER NINETEEN

CHARLIE CAREENED DOWN the muddy road, hands sweating, heart pounding, as she desperately drove to the little airport, trying to catch the plane that would take her to Kennedy Airport in New York City, which Trent was scheduled to fly out of in about ten hours. And, of course, the rain had begun the moment she'd left, slowing her progress and making it nearly impossible to get there in time.

But she had to get there. A simple phone call wasn't enough. She had to find Trent and tell him she loved him and beg him to forgive her.

As she'd thrown a few necessities into her suitcase and tried to process the whole, astonishing thing about his mother being a Gilchrist, and the unbelievable donation and phone call, she'd realized something else.

The fifty-thousand-dollar donation for the school must have come from Trent. Who else would just, out of the blue, anonymously donate that kind of money to their little school? The incredible realization made her see again what she'd come to know: that he was beyond extraordinary. A man with so much money, he could choose not to work at all. Instead, he'd trained for years to become a doctor and a specialized surgeon. He helped the poor and needy around the world, both financially and hands-on. He was adorable, funny, sweet and loved children. And if she didn't get to the airport on time, and find a way to make him forgive her, she'd never, ever meet anyone like him again.

She loved him and she'd hurt him. She'd tell him, show him, how much she loved him and make right all her wrongs.

She jammed her foot onto the accelerator. She had to get there and get on that plane. And if she didn't, she'd follow him to Florence or wherever else he was going. If she had to, she'd follow him to the moon.

Trent stretched his legs out in front of him and pulled his Panama hat down over his eyes. His flight from Kennedy was delayed, so he might as well try to sleep.

Except every time he closed his eyes he saw

Charlotte Grace Edwards. Never mind that there were five thousand miles between them, and that she'd lied and obviously didn't care about him the way he'd thought she did. Her face, her scent, her smile were all permanently etched in his brain and heart.

He'd broken his own damned rules and was paying the price for it. Knew he'd be paying the price for a long, long time.

He'd been happy with his life. He liked working in different places in the world, meeting new people, finding new medical challenges. Setting down roots in one place hadn't occurred to him until he'd gone to Liberia. Until he'd met Charlotte. Until she'd turned upside down everything he thought he knew about himself and what he wanted.

He hadn't gotten out fast enough. Their one-night fling had become something so much bigger, so much more important, so deeply painful. His vacation alone in Italy was going to be the worst weeks of his life, and his new job couldn't start soon enough.

A familiar, distinctive floral scent touched his nose, and to his disgust his heart slapped against his ribs and his breath shortened. Here he was, thinking about her so intently, so completely, he imagined she was near. Imagined he could touch her one last time.

Except the firm kick against his shoe wasn't his imagination.

He froze. Charlotte? Impossible.

"I know you're not asleep, Trent Dalton. Look at me."

Stunned, he slowly pushed his hat from his face and there she was. Or a mirage of her. He nearly extended his hand to see if she could possibly be real. He ran his gaze over every inch of her—her messy hair, her rumpled clothes, her bandaged arm.

She was real. The most real, the most beautiful woman he'd ever seen. His heart swelled and constricted at the same time, knowing what a damn fool he was to still feel that way.

"Why aren't you wearing the sling on your arm?"

She laughed, and the sound brought both joy and torment. "I nearly killed myself running off the road in a rainstorm to get to the airport, flew thousands of miles to find you, and the first thing you do is nag me?"

Yeah, she was something. He had to remind

himself that single-minded ruthlessness was part of the persona he'd adored. "What are you doing here, Charlotte?"

She crouched down in front of him, her green eyes suddenly deeply serious as they met his. "I came to apologize. I came to tell you how very sorry I am that I lied to you. That I realize no hospital wing, no donation, no amount of need, could possibly justify it, no matter how much I convinced myself it did."

It struck him that she'd gotten the Gilchrist donation, and that his mother had probably meddled and spilled the beans about who he was. Charlotte must somehow feel she had to apologize, to make it right, because of the money, even though it was an awful big trek for her to catch him here. His chest ached, knowing that was all this was.

"No need to apologize. I know the hospital means everything to you."

She slowly shook her head as her hand reached for his and squeezed, and his own tightened on hers when he should have pulled it away. "No, Trent. The hospital doesn't mean everything to me. I know that now."

"Well, pardon me when I say that's a line of bull. Like so many others you fed me." She'd already proven he couldn't trust anything she said. "You've shown you'll do anything to make things go your way for the place. You've shown it's your number-one priority over everything."

"Maybe it was. Maybe I let it be. But it isn't anymore." She stood and leaned forward, pressing a kiss to his mouth, and for a surprised moment he let himself feel it all the way to his soul. He let it fill all the cracks in his heart before he pulled away.

"You're my number-one priority, Trent. You're what means everything to me. Only you. I hated myself for lying to you. After you left, I hated myself even more for letting myself fall for you, because I was sure you'd just moved on to be with some woman in Italy. That I didn't mean anything to you but a brief good time."

"What makes you think that's not the case?" Though it was impossible to imagine how she could have believed that. That she hadn't seen the way he felt about her; hadn't known what she'd come to mean to him. But, if she didn't know, he sure as hell didn't want her to find out.

"Because I know you told Mike you wanted to be assigned to my little hospital for your year assignment." Tears filled her green eyes and he steeled himself against them; wouldn't be moved by them. "When I realized you'd left because of my stupid, misguided mistakes, I knew I had to do whatever I could to find you."

Obviously, she'd come because she still needed a plastic surgeon to get the hospital wing running. "You've found me. But my plane leaves in an hour, and I really don't want to go through a third goodbye. So please just go." The weight in his chest and balling in his stomach told him another goodbye might be even more painful than the second one in her kitchen, which he'd never have dreamed could be possible.

"No. No more goodbyes. I love you. I love you more than anything, and all I want is to be with you."

She loved him? He stared at her, wishing he could believe her. But he'd learned through a very hard lesson that she lied as easily as she breathed. He wasn't about to go back to Liberia with the woman who "loved" him only as long as she needed him to do plastic surgery work, or whatever the hell else was on her agenda, then doubtless wouldn't "love" him anymore.

"Sorry, Charlie, but I'm sure you can understand why I just don't believe you."

Tears welled in her eyes again. "You just called me Charlie," she whispered. "You're the only person who always calls me Charlotte."

He shrugged casually to show her none of this was affecting him the way it really was. "Maybe because you're not the person I thought you were."

He had to look away from the hurt in her eyes. "I hope I am the person you thought I was. Or at least that I can become that person. And I do understand why you don't believe me. I deserve that disbelief. I understand you need proof that I mean every word." Beneath her tears, her eyes sparked with the determined intensity he'd seen so often. "You once asked me why I went to Liberia to rebuild the hospital and school. And I told you my roots were dug in deep there, and I wanted to grow those roots, and I'd do it no matter what it takes. But I've changed my thoughts about that."

"How?"

"I'm not willing to do whatever it takes for the hospital, because that attitude led to some terrible mistakes. But I am willing to do whatever it takes to convince you I love you. That I want to grow roots with you and only you—wherever you choose to grow them. I always told you I can find doctors to work at the Edwards hospital, but not someone to run it. But you know what? I'm sure I *can* find someone to run it, and I will if you'll let me travel with you, be with you, help you, wherever it is you're headed."

He stared at her, stunned. The woman would be willing to leave the Edwards Mission Hospital to be with him instead? As much as he wanted to believe it, he couldn't. Her lies and machinations had been coldly calculated, and he had to wonder what exactly it was she was trying to achieve this time around. "No, Charlotte. You belong in Liberia and I belong wherever I am at a given moment."

"I belong with you, and I believe that you belong with me. I'm going to work hard to convince you how sorry I am for what I did. To give you so much love, you have to forgive me." She swiped away the tears on her lashes as her eyes flashed green sparks of determination. "You said I'm sometimes like a pit bull? You haven't seen anything yet. I'll get on the plane with you. I'll follow you wherever you go and keep asking you to forgive me and keep telling you how much I love you. I'm going to quit trying to control the world, like you always teased me about, and beg you to run it with me, for us to run it together. I want that because I love you. I love you and my life isn't complete without you."

He stared into her face. Would it be completely stupid of him to believe her again?

His heart pounded hard and he stood and looked down into her eyes focused so intently on his. In their depths, he saw very clearly what he was looking for.

Love. For him. It wasn't a lie. It was the truth.

He cupped her face in his hands and had to swallow past the lump that formed in his throat as he lowered his mouth to hers for a long kiss, absorbing the taste of her lips that he never thought he'd get to taste again.

"I love you too, Charlotte. I wish you'd just been honest with me but, standing here looking at you, I realize what you did doesn't matter if you really do love me. What matters is that I love you and you love me back." As he said the words, he knew with every ounce of his being it truly was the only thing that mattered. "Maybe if you'd told me, I would have left, I don't know. I do know that the way I felt about you scared the crap out of me."

"The way I felt about you scared me too. I knew you'd be out of my life in a matter of days, and it would be beyond stupid to fall in love with you. But I did anyway. I couldn't help it."

"Yeah?" Her words made him smile, because he'd felt exactly the same way. "I kept telling myself to keep my distance. But I found it impossible to resist a certain beautiful woman who tries to run the world." He tunneled his hands into her soft hair and looked into her eyes. "I've been running for a long time, Charlotte. I didn't really see it, until being with you made me look. But being with you made me realize that maybe, in all that running, I was really searching. And then I knew: I'd been searching for you."

A little sob left her throat and she flung her good arm around his neck. "Do you want me to come with you? Or would you like to go back to Liberia together? Will you live with me and work with me? Share my life with me?"

"I'm thinking heading back to Liberia is a good plan." He wrapped his arms around her, pressed his cheek to hers and smiled at the same time emotion clogged his chest. "So, is that a marriage proposal? Trust you not to let me be the one to ask."

"I'm sorry." She paused. "If we go back, I'll let you drive whenever you want."

He laughed out loud. "I'll believe that when I see it. And yes, Charlotte Grace Edwards, I'll marry you and live with you and work with you for the rest of our lives." He lowered his mouth to hers and whispered against her lips. "This is the last time you have to drag me back from an airport. This time, I'm staying for good."

* * * * *

Mills & Boon® Large Print
Medical

November

200 HARLEY STREET: THE PROUD ITALIAN   Alison Roberts
200 HARLEY STREET: AMERICAN SURGEON   Lynne Marshall
IN LONDON
A MOTHER'S SECRET   Scarlet Wilson
RETURN OF DR MAGUIRE   Judy Campbell
SAVING HIS LITTLE MIRACLE   Jennifer Taylor
HEATHERDALE'S SHY NURSE   Abigail Gordon

December

200 HARLEY STREET: THE SOLDIER PRINCE   Kate Hardy
200 HARLEY STREET: THE ENIGMATIC SURGEON   Annie Claydon
A FATHER FOR HER BABY   Sue MacKay
THE MIDWIFE'S SON   Sue MacKay
BACK IN HER HUSBAND'S ARMS   Susanne Hampton
WEDDING AT SUNDAY CREEK   Leah Martyn

January

200 HARLEY STREET: THE SHAMELESS MAVERICK   Louisa George
200 HARLEY STREET: THE TORTURED HERO   Amy Andrews
A HOME FOR THE HOT-SHOT DOC   Dianne Drake
A DOCTOR'S CONFESSION   Dianne Drake
THE ACCIDENTAL DADDY   Meredith Webber
PREGNANT WITH THE SOLDIER'S SON   Amy Ruttan

Mills & Boon® Large Print
Medical

February

TEMPTED BY HER BOSS	Scarlet Wilson
HIS GIRL FROM NOWHERE	Tina Beckett
FALLING FOR DR DIMITRIOU	Anne Fraser
RETURN OF DR IRRESISTIBLE	Amalie Berlin
DARING TO DATE HER BOSS	Joanna Neil
A DOCTOR TO HEAL HER HEART	Annie Claydon

March

A SECRET SHARED...	Marion Lennox
FLIRTING WITH THE DOC OF HER DREAMS	Janice Lynn
THE DOCTOR WHO MADE HER LOVE AGAIN	Susan Carlisle
THE MAVERICK WHO RULED HER HEART	Susan Carlisle
AFTER ONE FORBIDDEN NIGHT...	Amber McKenzie
DR PERFECT ON HER DOORSTEP	Lucy Clark

April

IT STARTED WITH NO STRINGS...	Kate Hardy
ONE MORE NIGHT WITH HER DESERT PRINCE...	Jennifer Taylor
FLIRTING WITH DR OFF-LIMITS	Robin Gianna
FROM FLING TO FOREVER	Avril Tremayne
DARE SHE DATE AGAIN?	Amy Ruttan
THE SURGEON'S CHRISTMAS WISH	Annie O'Neil